EION

CYBORG ROGUES

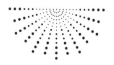

ALYSE ANDERS

Eion – Cyborg Rogues

Copyright 2021 Alyse Anders

ISBN: 978-1-990064-05-0

All Rights Are Reserved.

No part of this book may be used or reproduced in any manner whatsoever without written permission, except in the case of brief quotations embodied in critical articles and reviews.

This is a work of fiction. All of the characters, organizations, and events portrayed in this story are either products of the author's imagination or are used fictitiously, and any resemblance to actual events, locales or persons, living or dead, is entirely coincidental.

Publisher: Alyse Anders www.alyseanders.com

Cover Design: Alyse Anders

Images: https://www.depositphotos.com

First edition: April 2021

THE BLACK GUARD

As far as the Black Guard were concerned, everything was going according to plan.

The Grus were a race of peacekeepers, innovators, and when necessary, enforcers. For centuries, their people were the guiding light in their quadrant of space, ensuring that those who wanted to take advantage of weaker races couldn't do so.

People like the Black Guard.

When the Grus had been attacked by the Sholle – a silent, malevolent race who traveled planet to planet stripping them bare of natural resources before leaving – their world was nearly destroyed, and their people sacrificed everything to stop them. A brilliant scientist created a cybernetic matrix which allowed for those who'd died on the battlefield to be reborn as the Fallen, a new cybernetic race of super soldiers who were finally able to defeat the Sholle.

To protect the remnants of their world and to rebuild their society, the Grus withdrew in on themselves, cutting off contact with the other races. Gone were the protectors of the quadrant, the strongest force who'd served as mediators and ensured peace between the races was maintained.

The Black Guard saw the void left by the Grus and knew this was their chance.

The Grus aren't here to keep you safe, but we are. Let us help you, let us protect you. No, no, it won't cost you much. Just some credits. Some extra goods. Here's one of our men to help you.

It's fine.

You're fine.

We'll keep you safe.

Except they didn't. The greater the number of Black Guard operatives arriving on planets to take positions within the various corporations and governments of the quadrant, the tighter their grip on power became. By the time anyone realized what was happening, it was too late. They now controlled the governments, businesses, and essential services, taking all the profits for themselves and leaving the citizens to suffer. Then the Black Guard would move on to the next planet.

Criminals? Us? Not at all.

You simply owe us a debt and you wouldn't want to renege on that.

Would you?

Oh, everything was going perfectly well. They were patient, infiltrating every key area, ensuring that the debts owed to them were pervasive and insurmountable. All they needed was time to ensure that no one would escape their grasp.

Then the unthinkable happened.

A ship arrived from the depths of space bringing a group of twenty-eight women. These were no ordinary women, but rather the mates of the Fallen whose very presence changed the balance of power in the quadrant. The Fallen, once ostracized by the Grus, were welcomed home, a people cleaved in two finally whole. The Grus were back, more powerful for their reunification with the Fallen, and ready to reclaim their place as protectors.

The Black Guard wasn't about to let that happen.

The humans were a threat greater to their hold on power than anything they'd faced before now. They were also the Fallen's greatest weakness. If the women could be captured, converted, or killed, well then, the Fallen would be at the mercy of the Black Guard. The balance of power would be flipped once more, and all would be righted.

All they needed to do was to capture the humans.

Simple.

CHAPTER ONE

Eion stepped out into the damp and cold night as the wind gusted against his face. The near-freezing temperatures wouldn't hurt him, but it was a stark reminder of all that had happened to his people and his planet. The Grus people lived on a space station orbiting Zarlan, while the Fallen did the best they could on the planet below.

Turning, he made his way through the empty streets, hidden from the Fallen, Grus, and now as a small number of humans who lived in the city. With the wind as strong as it was tonight, he knew there was little chance anyone would see, let alone care about a lone cyborg out for a walk. But old habits were hard to shake.

The weather patterns on Zarlan had been harsh ever since the Sholle had attacked over fifty years ago, stripping their planet of nearly all their natural resources and leaving them with barely enough to sustain life on the surface. The Fallen didn't care. This was their home, the one that they'd died and been reborn to protect, the one that was now in their care and their responsibility to try and resurrect.

Not that he was a scientist or had any skills that he could help to bring life back to the lifeless surface. No, Eion was a soldier, a killer. His purpose had been to protect, to drive out all those who'd wanted to hurt his people and for far too long he'd sat idly by with little to do.

The communicator in his hand was an uncomfortable weight as he walked to the meeting point. He turned the device over and over in his grip as though the action would be enough to give him the answers he hadn't realized he'd been seeking. He'd woken to find the device sitting by the door inside the small apartment he'd been holed up in for the past few months. Eion knew there were very few people who would not only be able to track him down, but stupid enough to break into his home and leave something for him unannounced. That meant Gadiel had found him, and if he'd resurfaced then there was something significant happening.

Eion hated not knowing what that was.

During the war with the Sholle, his elite squad – the Qadrus – had been sent into some of the most harrowing nests to dispatch the Sholle within. Before every mission, Gadiel provided Eion with every detail so together they could strategize effectively. Gadiel might have been their leader, the one who took responsibility for the outcome of each mission, but it was Eion's duty and his plans that safeguarded their squad and guaranteed that each of them had everything they needed to achieve victory. If there was a blank spot in their information, Eion would suss it out, knowing that the details ensured their success and brought them one step closer to defeating the Sholle – and saving the Grus.

But the war was long over and Eion had nothing left to cling to, no purpose to keep him focused. He'd wandered the surface of Zarlan, helping where he could. He'd often spend his time drinking vast amounts of *cashata,* hoping that perhaps this time the nanobots wouldn't be able to keep up with the alcohol, and he'd finally reach the blessed state of inebriation so he could forget for just a little while.

It never worked.

There'd only been one message on the communicator when he'd picked it up – *At the drop point* – which was the order Gadiel used whenever they were to be deployed. It was something Eion hadn't seen in nearly forty years, not since they'd been dispatched to clean up the messes left behind by the Sholle, the remaining horrors that few others knew. The moment he read the words, years of training clicked back into place and he was able to push down the pain and guilt that had comprised his life for so long. He could finally be useful again.

The night did little to conceal things from his cybernetic eyes. Upon reaching the location, he took a moment to scan the area using every spectrum his enhanced vision and sensors allowed. Every nook and cranny were visible to him, open for him to catalogue and ensure no one who shouldn't be present was here. The fact he couldn't detect the others meant nothing, given their abilities to conceal their bio signatures. It wasn't quite time for them to meet, so they all remained hidden.

Eion continued to turn the communicator in his hand until it finally let out a single soft beep. There they were. Stepping out into the empty square, the wind battering his long jacket, Eion let his gaze fall upon the men who were as close to him as brothers.

Gadiel, Weixler, Qwin and himself; enforcers, hunters, cyborgs sent out into their quadrant of space to ensure no one would ever harm the Grus, the Fallen, or their planet ever again.

Gadiel looked at each of them and Eion couldn't help but wonder what his leader and friend had been doing in the years since they'd last seen one another. He looked older, something that shouldn't be possible with the nanobots in his bloodstream, and far more tired than Eion would have thought. But there was something else, something that he never would have anticipated.

Gadiel looked the tiniest bit excited.

Thank you for coming. Gadiel used the special cybernetic channel that had been created only for the four of them. *It has been far too long since I've seen you all.*

It's not like we were doing anything. Weixler shook his head, frowning. *You could have reached out.*

Eion couldn't help but roll his eyes. *You know full well none of us would have come. We've been collectively sulking since the war ended and we lost our purpose.*

Speak for yourself, Wex. Qwin was always the most optimistic of their group. *I've been busy working with Hallam coordinating a satellite medical facility for the far side of Zarlan. Lots to do if you want to involve yourself.*

That had always been the problem for Eion, knowing what to do with the skills he'd developed during the war. There hadn't been much need for a killer in recent years. Though in the past several months he'd noticed a change in the air. Something different had descended upon his people, and he got the feeling he was about to discover exactly what the details were. *Why are we here, Gad?*

Gadiel looked at each of them, as though he were trying to ascertain something. *Do any of you have an itching in the back of your brain?*

Eion stiffened and felt the collective shock from the others through their link. *How did you know that?*

It's been fraking driving me insane for months now. Weixler's purple eyes flashed, sending deep shadows across his dark skin. *I thought I was being decommissioned somehow.*

Hallam had asked me something similar weeks ago, but I'd ignored him. Qwin stepped closer to the center of the square they'd formed. *What's wrong with us?*

Gadiel held up his hands. *Nothing is wrong. Not really. Things have simply gotten more ... complicated.*

Eion waited for him to continue, knowing Gadiel was trying to find the right words. He always did that, never wanting to misrepresent the situation or lead them down the wrong path. *I'm going to assume you've heard about the humans.*

Only a fool wouldn't have known about the Kraken, the ship that had somehow crossed the vastness of space without weapons or shields, bringing a small group of humans with it. Eion had been fascinated by the story, though he couldn't be sure that all the rumors he'd heard were true. That said, the arrival had prompted increased security on Grus Prime, and then at the medical facility on Zarlan. He'd assumed that the humans had something wrong with them, something that certain individuals were trying to contain. *I take it the humans brought an infection of some sort with them. Do they need us to do something about it?* He hated the idea of killing a group of people for something that could be outside their control.

Not in the manner that you're assuming. Gadiel slipped his hands into the deep pockets of his waist length jacket. *That buzzing is indicative of a connection that each of us has with one of the humans.*

What connection? Qwin narrowed his gaze. *Do not all Fallen respond to their presence with the itching? Why did Hallam keep this from me? I've been in constant contact with him even since the arrival of the ship.*

No, it's not all Fallen. Gadiel took a breath. *Apparently, when the females are woken up it causes some of us to...lose control. They're our mates.*

Eion stared hard at Gadiel, unable to process what he'd said. *That's impossible.*

Qwin took another step forward. *Our emotions were taken from us when our matrixes were installed. There's no way for us to connect to another being in any manner that's not rooted in anger and vengeance. We all know that. What kind of lives are these women going to have, being forced to spend it with members of our kind?*

Weixler's growl rivaled the howling wind. *They should be sent to live on Grus Prime. There's no life for them on Zarlan.*

Eion couldn't imagine what the humans' lives had been like for them to leave their planet and cross the vastness of space the way that they had, but they didn't deserve to be put into any sort of relationship with a Fallen.

Mates? What a horrible fate to befall them.

I've been in contact with Rykal. Gadiel strode over to the wall of the closest building and pressed his back to it. *Those of us impacted are the first twenty-eight Fallen to have been reborn. They still don't understand why, but the women were called to us, drawn here for reasons that no one can quite determine. Once the mating happens, the Fallen are changed. I wouldn't have believed it if I hadn't been connected to Rykal through the link. I felt the differences in him.*

Eion hadn't met Rykal in person. The leader of the Fallen needed to have plausible deniability when it came to some of their more sensitive missions, and as a result it was safer for everyone if Rykal kept his distance. He knew Gadiel spoke with him often as they were provided directives, some of which came as a back channel from Grus Prime, the space station that orbited Zarlan and was the new home for the Grus. If he said that the leader of the Fallen had changed, then Eion believed him.

Still, the thought of having a mate didn't sit right with him. *What have these women to say about the situation?*

Nothing. They've been kept in stasis until Hallam and the others were able to determine a safe way to wake more than one of them at once. They believe they've found a solution to that problem and want to test it out in a controlled environment.

Weixler snorted. *We're to be test subjects once again.*

Except this time something good will be there waiting for us on the other side. Gadiel looked once more at each of them. *Don't you think its finally time for us to receive a prize, something for ourselves after all the years of service that we've given? Even if this isn't exactly what you'd hoped for, why should we say no?*

Eion hadn't considered the idea of having a mate. The Fallen weren't exactly busting with softer emotions, nothing to draw them to one of their own kind, and until the recent reunification with the Grus, they'd been little more than outcasts with the people who they'd once called their own. Anger and rage had been what fueled him in life, and the idea of anything more than that was a foreign concept Eion couldn't fathom.

Gadiel pushed away from the wall. *This isn't an order, I can't force any of you to do anything, but I want you to come with me to the medical facility. I'm asking that you allow Hallam to test his theory and let the human women wake from their stasis.*

Qwin nodded. *Yes.*

What will happen to the women if we say no? Of course, it was Weixler to ask that.

I can't say for sure, but it would not be fair to just leave them in stasis forever.

Weixler held Gadiel in his gaze, nodding to affirm his consent.

Gadiel continued to explain the details. *Apparently, our reaction is so strong that it causes chaos, overrides our logic and control. It's too dangerous to wake the women without their mate being restrained.*

Eion and the others received a flash of a memory from Gadiel, but one that wasn't his own. Rykal kidnapping a small, red headed woman with pale skin and leaving Grus Prime in an escape pod. Possessive infatuation and something Eion could only assume was love flowed through the memory as though the emotions belonged to Eion himself. If someone as controlled and responsible as Rykal responded in such a way, risking full-on war with the Grus, then he had no doubt the concerns they'd have if someone far less moderate were set off.

I'll come. Eion had no reason not to. *Come on, Wex. Aren't you the least bit curious to know what kind of woman would travel across space to mate with your sorry ass?*

When Weixler couldn't hide his smirk, Eion knew he had him. *She'll have to be insane. That could be fun.*

Gadiel turned and strode down the street, knowing full well each of them quickly fell into step behind him. Eion wasn't sure exactly what was going to happen in the next few hours, but for the first time since before his rebirth, he felt something other than anger.

He was hopeful.

CHAPTER TWO

The four of them stood in a large room, surrounded by medical equipment and personnel who spent more time casting curious glances at them than the readings on their machines. If Eion hadn't known about the nature of how Fallen responded to their human mates, he would have suspected something was wrong by the others' reactions alone. Not to mention the room had security features that would easily incapacitate them all if something went wrong.

Eion couldn't imagine the carnage that would ensue if the four of them lost their minds.

Hallam, the head of the medical facility and the man responsible for ensuring the humans were safe, entered the room. "Everyone leave."

The staff quickly finished their scans and fled as though a Sholle were about to enter the room. Hallam waited for them to leave before turning his attention to them. "I'm not going to use the cybernetic link for communication. Once I inject you with the compound, you might each find that your matrix functionality has been muted. Don't panic as this is to be expected."

"Hello to you too, Hallam." Gadiel's voice was flat, devoid of any hint of sarcasm. "Thank you for being so hospitable."

"Let's be clear about what is happening." Hallam straightened, letting his gaze linger on each of them. "I didn't want the first test group to be your squad. I'd hoped we'd be able to try the dampening agent on Fallen who had the potential to be far less deadly than you. But I need to be able to monitor and evaluate the interactions between a group to see if there's anything that might cause multiples to lose control faster, or if your connection will ensure you're able to maintain hold on your control longer. You're the only group of Fallen who've worked this closely together, so like it or not I'm stuck with you."

Eion felt Hallam's annoyance even without the benefit of the cybernetic link. The Qadrus was known for their covert missions, skirting the rules to their benefit to help protect the Grus and keep the Fallen secured. Individually, they were some of the deadliest soldiers that had been created for the war. Together, they were a terrifyingly effective force. As a doctor, Hallam was responsible for the preservation of life, it would be logical that he'd take exception to their purpose.

Qwin stepped forward, placing a hand on Hallam's shoulder when he got close. "My friend, I know you, I know how hard you've worked to keep us all safe over the decades. We've all had our roles to play, whether it was a chosen calling, or one that was forced upon us. The war is over, and we'd like the opportunity to have lives that don't involve death around every corner."

Even the idea of having a life like what he'd lived before the war. Before he'd died on the battlefield and been reborn as a cyborg, only to be placed back into the heart of the battle, well that was so foreign to Eion he wasn't certain what it even meant. What was *normal*? The days and nights he spent on his own, alone, reading reports of the immediate sectors that surrounded Zarlan and Grus Prime. He could leave Zarlan, but off planet their kind was shunned just as much by races other than the

Grus. Isolation had been his version of normal for so long, Eion knew of no other life.

Normal.

Normal for whom?

Gadiel cast a glance his way, but Eion refused to meet it.

"How is this going to work?" Qwin patted Hallam on the shoulder once more before moving back to join the rest of them.

"I'm going to run a scan of your brains and matrixes to see what the bio signature and brainwave patterns show. I also need to ensure all of your cybernetics are functioning properly, so we don't have any unexpected reactions. We have all the humans still in stasis and are monitoring their responses. What we've observed in the past is a harmonization of those patterns the closer you are to your mate. That's what I believe the itching in the back of your brains is. Synchronization."

Yes, if nothing else, getting rid of that damned itching would be a blessing. Weixler crossed his arms, his purple eyes flashing. "After the scans, you locate the women, inject us and then what? Wait to see if we lose our collective minds and tear this place apart? That doesn't sound wise."

"If I didn't have confidence in the science or the quality of my work, you wouldn't be here." The edge in Hallam's voice sharpened. "You might find this hard to believe, but this isn't all about you. These women have been in stasis for far longer than they should have. The equipment that's currently sustaining their lives is old and I'm fearful that it's going to start breaking down. I'm not willing to let any of them die, but I'm equally not willing to let the remaining Fallen mates run wild trying to get to them. We need to solve this problem as quickly as we can so we can all move on with our lives."

Qwin rubbed the back of his head. "I suggest we get started."

Gadiel nodded his agreement. "Do what you need to, Hallam. We're here to help."

"Stand still while I complete the scans. It won't take long but we will still need to track down which women are being impacted by your presence." Hallam moved behind them, running the scanner along the back of their matrixes. "I'm pleased none of you have responded stronger to their presence. That means the shielding I put in place is functioning better. The last time I brought a Fallen mate here, he nearly lost his mind." The scanner bleeped its completion and Hallam marched past them and out of the room.

The sound of the doors being secured behind him sent a small shiver of panic through Eion. They were safe here, but he'd never been fond of situations where he didn't have an obvious escape route. Still, there was something strange about his response to everything, as though while his logic and reasoning wanted him to fall back onto his training, there was a growing part of him that knew there was no way he'd ever leave this building without taking his mate with him.

Now that he was aware of her presence, he knew that there was a reason for the itching, for the unsettled sensations that had been picking at his brain for months now. He wanted nothing more than for everything to come to a point so he could resolve matters once and for all. What kind of woman would leave her home for an unknown future? She must be brave, a trait he admired immensely.

Looking down at his cybernetic arm, he couldn't help but wonder what she'd think of him.

Eion had died at the height of the war with the Sholle, staying at Gadiel's side when it was clear that their mission was doomed to fail. They'd been trying to make their way into one of the Sholle transport ships, to infiltrate and convert it into a weapon that could be used against its creators. They'd nearly succeeded.

He'd been terrified when they'd found a conduit large enough to allow them to enter the ship but didn't hesitate to climb inside, knowing failure wasn't something they could afford. The narrow winding passageway should have led them straight into the engineering section of the ship. They'd double checked the schematics, everything should have been perfect – and yet, when they'd gotten halfway to their goal, they'd tripped a security sensor that wasn't on the plans. They'd barely made it back out of the ship, when the Sholle spotted them.

Eion didn't remember dying.

It was the pain of his rebirth, the implantation of his cybernetic matrix that was forever seared into his memory. The all-encompassing agony that filled his veins as his consciousness was yanked back from the abyss and forced to confront his new painful reality. Aidric, the creator of the matrix, had been there, his eyes full of compassion and regret as Eion's rebirth was completed. A brief explanation of what had happened, a check of his new systems and then on a shuttle heading back to Zarlan's surface.

Once more, he was forced to fight.

Looking at the still closed doors, he couldn't help but wonder again if this apparent mating bond was his reward for his sacrifices. Did the universe work in such a way? Who was he to think himself worthy of such a prize?

No, this was no doubt another strange trick of life, something that on the surface appeared to be a joy but would inevitably turn into a painful reminder of how harsh life could be.

"What kind of race do you think these humans are?" Weixler's voice was far softer than normal. "Who would want to be mated with the likes of us?"

"They've got an edge to them." Qwin crossed his arms and widened his stance. "Can you imagine a group of Grus females boarding a shuttle, going into stasis and hoping to survive?"

Gadiel chuckled. "I wouldn't go disparaging our females. I know more than a few who'd take great pleasure in dismantling your cybernetics for even hinting at their lack of abilities."

"That's the problem. They're not our females any longer." Weixler strode over to the computer monitor but stopped to only stare at it. "The Grus didn't care about us after the war, so why should I care about them now?"

"Unification. That's the reason you should care." Qwin's eternal optimism was only mildly annoying. "We've come so far in such a short period of time. Both our people need to put aside our differences so we can finally move forward."

Weixler grunted. "You sound like Rykal."

"There are worse people to be compared to than our leader."

Eion was about to say something when an overwhelming panic slammed into him. He dropped to his knees as his matrix flooded with sensations. She was awake, she was so close he could almost smell her body. His cock pulsed with life for the first time since his rebirth, as arousal coursed through his veins.

"Eion?" Gadiel was at his side, his hand pressed to the back of Eion's neck. "What's happening?"

There was no way he could answer, the ability to form words currently beyond his capabilities. Not when he felt her fear and confusion washing over him, her concern for someone other than herself. She was fighting whatever was happening to her, needing to make sure someone...who was that...was okay.

He needed to get to her. She needed his help, and he wasn't there, *frak* he had to find his way out of here so he could protect her.

Eion tried to move, but Gadiel held him in place. It was then that he realized Hallam had returned and was trying to speak to him. There were words, concern, but none of it mattered to him.

There was only her.

The press of the injector to the back of his neck barely registered, but within seconds Eion was able to take a breath and close his eyes. The rush of emotions slowly began to recede, making it easier for him to finally regain a small measure of control.

"Are you okay?" Hallam was close enough that Eion felt his breath on his face.

"No." It was difficult to swallow past the tightness of his throat. "Better than I was."

"That's all I can hope for at this point." Hallam got to his feet as Gadiel helped Eion into a sitting position. "The rest of you need the injections now. The other women will be coming out of stasis soon, and I don't want a repeat of what Eion just went through."

Eion could only watch as Hallam administered the injections and each of his squad grabbed the backs of their heads. The creeping insanity that had threatened to overwhelm him had diminished enough he could focus his attention on *her* and what she was feeling.

She was scared, but not for herself. Confused about what was happening but focused on protecting someone. Eion needed to go to her, to reassure her that everything was going to be okay, that they were all safe now. The impulse to move was so strong he nearly couldn't stop himself from crawling across the floor.

Letting out a loud groan, he pressed his forehead to the floor. "Is she okay? I thought you were waiting to wake them until we'd been injected?"

"I'm sorry." Hallam was back at his side, kneeling on the floor. "I have an overenthusiastic assistant who triggered the stasis cycle on your mate before we were ready. The others will be woken once Aerin receives my signal."

Eion lifted his head and met Hallam's gaze. "Is she okay?"

"Yes. She's worried about her sister who is also one of the other mates. Aerin had to inject her with the nanobots far faster than I would have liked so we could explain the situation. Your mate handled it surprisingly well. These humans are a resilient bunch."

Good. He didn't want her to worry or be scared, not when Eion wasn't able to do anything to help her yet. "When can we get out of here and see them?"

"Not yet. I need to ensure that the rest of your squad is under control before I can risk bringing them up."

Hallam cocked his head to the side in the manner that many of them did when communicating with another Fallen through their cybernetic link. Normally, Eion would have been alerted to the communication but something was blocking his ability to reach out. Shifting his attention toward Gadiel, he attempted to connect to him through the link. "I can't reach anyone."

"As I said, that was to be expected." Hallam stood, helping Eion to his feet. "We needed to dampen the connection as much as we could if we wanted to keep control of your reactions." He looked the rest of them over, scanning them as he went. "Aerin is bringing the rest of your mates out of stasis now and once I'm certain you're all under control, she'll escort them here to meet you."

The tension inside Eion eased once again. He could still feel her and her emotional state, but he was able to keep control of his impulses. Soon she'd be here, and they wouldn't have to worry about anything else. He'd be able to see her face and know that for the first time in a long while his life wouldn't be filled with hardship, pain, and loneliness.

Without being told, Eion knew the moment the other women had begun their awakening out of stasis. The others groaned nearly all at once and he saw their physical reactions to the strength of their connection with these women, their mates. With their injections given to them before the awakenings, their responses were far more muted than what he'd experienced. Hallam watched them all closely and it was only then that Eion remembered he'd already gone through this with his own mate, and he'd lacked the benefit of any assistance.

"How did you manage?" The question was from him before he really thought about it.

Hallam's gaze slipped away. "I nearly didn't."

Time passed slowly as the women were pulled from stasis and

the others became increasingly aware of every aspect of their presence. They occasionally shared looks, but Eion knew they all felt the same as him – the only thing that mattered was having them brought here so they could finally be together. Weixler was clearly agitated and knowing him the way Eion did, he wouldn't be able to hold back for long.

Finally, he felt her coming closer. They were on their way here and he'd finally be able to see what color her eyes were, what her hair smelled like. He moved closer to the door, ignoring the soft growl that escaped Qwin, knowing that he was between him and his mate. Eion didn't give a *frak*.

She was coming.

CHAPTER THREE

From the moment Kaia opened her eyes, she knew something strange was happening. When she'd slid into the stasis tube back on Earth, the last person she'd seen was Captain Lena McGovern of the Kraken, the long-haul transport ship that was taking them into space. Lena was a bubbly sort but oozed competence and determination, which was all the reassurance Kaia had needed to sign herself and her sister up for this journey into the unknown. Kaia had expected to see Lena when she opened her eyes – that had been the agreement after all – a familiar sight to reassure her that everything was okay, and they'd reached a safe port.

Her breath caught in her throat when her vision began to clear, and instead of Lena's red hair and wide smile, she was staring up into a strange woman's glowing brown eyes, her face partially covered with cybernetic implants.

"What the fuck!" Kaia tried to move but the stasis tube was still partially engaged making it nearly impossible to get free.

The woman jerked her hands up and away. "No one is going to hurt you." Her Earth standard wasn't as smooth as Kaia was used to hearing but given that she was obviously not of human origin, the fact that she spoke it at all was a small miracle. "My name is Aerin. Your ship has safely landed on our planet and all the passengers are unharmed."

Olya!

"I need to see my sister." The top of the stasis tube had mostly retracted at this point, giving her room to kick her feet at the tubes and wires that had moved during their journey. "Where is she?"

"Your sister is still in stasis. She's safe and well taken care of." Aerin's short blonde hair had slipped forward, covering part of her eyes. "I need you to calm yourself. Your body needs time to adjust to being awake once more."

"Where's Lena?" Kaia sat up too quickly, sending a wave of nausea over her. "Shit."

"Breathe. Slow and deep. That's it." Aerin moved closer and ran what appeared to be a scanner across Kaia's body. "Lena is on her way. One of the assistants accidently woke you before we were ready, and I had no choice but to continue the process. I apologize for that."

The simple act of breathing was enough to help stem the rising panic that threatened to overwhelm her. Clearly, everything was okay for the time being. They'd survived their journey through the perils of deep space and had somehow managed to find a friendly species who'd agreed to help them. The odds of everything going this perfectly, well, were astronomical. That meant they'd probably used up all their good luck getting here, and she'd have to keep her eyes open for things going wrong.

Because in her experience, things always went wrong.

Aerin continued to speak to the others around her in their own language, while continuing to monitor whatever she was seeing on the data pad in front of her. "You're one of four women that we will be bringing out of stasis. Once you're all awake, I will answer the questions you no doubt have for me."

"Is my sister one of the others you're waking? If not, she needs to be on that list. I'm not doing anything or going anywhere without her with me."

Olya was the reason they'd embarked on this journey to nowhere in the first place, and Kaia needed to know that she was okay. Stasis was only going to hold the Breneman's virus back for so long. Kaia could only hope this place and these people were medically advanced enough to be able to offer if not a cure, then at least a treatment that would postpone the inevitable.

Aerin pressed a series of buttons on her data pad. "Your sister is identified as Olyana in the passenger manifest."

"Olya, yeah that's her."

"Then yes, she's one of the four. Though I see she has also been flagged as having a disease." Aerin's eyebrows shot up, a flash momentarily brightening her glowing eyes. "She'll need to immediately be injected with nanobots to correct the problem. We can't have a foreign illness being introduced to our sector of space."

"Fine. Yes, whatever you need to do." Kaia closed her eyes and for the briefest of moments she let herself believe that everything might end up being okay for them.

Thank god.

Kaia did her best to try and keep relaxed, but there was something off with herself. Her brain felt a bit sluggish, and her emotions were suddenly all over the place, making it difficult for her to concentrate on what was happening around her. It was as though she were being watched by someone just out of sight, but she was only peripherally aware of their presence. There were many people who looked like Aerin scurrying around the four stasis tubes that were in the room. Where the remainder of the Kraken's passengers were, Kaia hadn't a clue. She'd figure that out as soon as she knew Olya was going to be okay.

Her stasis tube finally disengaged, and Kaia was able to slowly get out and onto her feet for the first time in...well, she didn't know. Based on how her muscles shook and her feet ached, it had been quite some time. Aerin was back by her side when she tried to take a step and nearly fell to the floor.

"I know you want to see your sister, but I need to inject you with some nanobots first. They will help ease your recovery and will act as a translation device for the alien races you're about to encounter."

"I should have known it wasn't luck that you were speaking an Earth language."

Aerin smiled softly. "No. I've taken some time now to learn enough of your language to help wake your people. Lena can't always be here to assist and the nanobots require an explanation before I inject them."

The thought of having alien tech inserted into her bloodstream should have freaked Kaia the fuck out, but she'd come too far and sacrificed too much to stop now. "What do I need to know?"

"Initially when they were injected into Lena and the first few humans, the nanobots elicited a strong physical reaction. It was painful and caused nausea. We've since made modifications, adjusted for human physiology, but I still want you to be aware in case the adjustment doesn't work as anticipated."

"Fair enough." Kaia was glad she'd be getting the injection before Olya. It would be easier to walk her sister through the process if she had firsthand experience. "And these nanobots will help my sister's illness?"

"Yes. It might not be instant, but they should make the necessary repairs to her body." She held up the injector for Kaia to see. "I can start with you if you'd like, or we can wait until the others are conscious before we begin. I leave the decision with you."

As tempting as it was to jump in feet first and get the injection now, she knew it would probably benefit the others if they were awake to bear witness. "I'll go first once the others are out of stasis."

"As you wish." Aerin tucked the injector into her pocket. "Why don't you sit here so you can watch."

There was a chair off to the side, still in line of sight of everything that was happening, but out of the way enough that she wouldn't be a bother. Kaia wasn't exactly known for remaining on the sidelines when shit was going down, especially when family was involved. But her head ached, and her legs were far too wobbly for her to stand on them for long, making her more of an obstacle than an asset. She allowed Aerin to guide her over to the seat and tried to relax as much as she could. "Which one is Olya's?"

"This one." Aerin pointed to the tube closest to her. "We'll wake her up next."

Okay good, fine. She could wait a bit longer to know that her sister was going to be okay. That her insane idea for packing them up and going out into the middle of space, leaving their family behind to never see or hear from again, wasn't going to be for nothing. Because that had been the one thing that had been eating at the back of her mind from the moment she'd learned about the Kraken and Lena's plan to leave Earth. She couldn't live with herself if they'd sacrificed everything they'd ever known, only to fail and Olya die anyway.

Kaia could only sit and stare as Aerin and the others began the wake cycle of the stasis tubes. Alarms, beeps, and alien voices shouting sent a chill through her, causing her stomach to flip. *Keep calm, everything's going to be okay. Olya will be fine.* She'd lie to herself if necessary, but Kaia had to hold at least a little faith that for once things would work out for them.

The doors off to the side opened and a large man with long black hair, glowing eyes, and two cybernetic arms strode into the room. Kaia could only assume he was the one in charge based on how everyone around him responded. She didn't know how, but he must have been able to communicate with them without speaking, due to the change in direction that some of the others made. He stopped in front of Aerin, who immediately looked her way. His eyes flashed briefly before he strode over to her. Kaia's heart raced at the intensity of his presence and the air of confidence he exuded.

"I'm Hallam. I'm the doctor here." His Earth standard wasn't as crisp as Aerin's, holding far heavier an accent. "Stay with Aerin. Listen to her."

"Okay." Before she had a chance to say anything else, he turned and raced from the room. "That doesn't sound good."

"He wasn't prepared for you to be awake yet." Aerin let out a small growl. "We needed to coordinate better."

"What did you need to coordinate with? We're all right here." Unless there was something else going on in this facility that she was unaware of, she couldn't imagine four women coming out a stasis would pose much of a problem for them.

Aerin turned and pointed to her assistants. "There's still much you don't know about our world. We're taking a risk waking more than one of you at a time."

"What risk? You all seem to have cybernetics which means you're far stronger than we would be. I can't imagine we'd be able to overpower you at all."

"You're not our concern." Cocking her head to the side, she pointed to the other stasis tubes, sending several smaller teams into action. "We need to ensure the others aren't woken before Hallam is prepared."

Kaia could only watch as the teams got into position, pressing buttons, and monitoring readings on screens she couldn't quite see. Her brain raced trying to figure out exactly what they were coordinating and what the threat was they had to mitigate. If they were walking into a dangerous situation, Kaia needed to know to ensure she was ready and able to keep Olya safe.

"Do I have a reason to be worried here?" She leaned forward, resting her elbows on her knees as another wave of nausea hit her. "I'm not sure I'm able to physically run anywhere if that's a thing that needs to happen."

"You and the others won't be harmed." Aerin said, looking back at Kaia over her shoulder. "Patience, please."

"I'm not exactly known for that." She also didn't know how trusting she should be given the circumstances. "Who are you worried about?"

Aerin didn't have time to respond as she straightened and waved at the others who triggered the revival procedure. The three stasis tubes hissed their covers open, revealing the precious cargo held within. Kaia got to her feet and carefully made her way over to Olya's tube, relieved as she saw the colour of her sister's face start to change from grey to something closer to normal. Lena had been more than a little concerned about how Olya would manage for a long period in stasis, and Kaia had to ignore her own fears. When Olya opened her eyes and smiled up at her, Kaia was finally able to relax.

"Hey." Her voice cracked from the rush of emotions. "There you are."

"Hey." Olya cringed. "Throat's sore."

"Yeah, it takes a little bit for everything to get working again. Take your time and everything will be fine."

"How long? Where?"

Those were questions she still had herself. "We'll get all that information in a little bit. Right now, we just need to wake you up and get you on your feet."

"Okay."

Kaia looked up to see the other two women start to move in their tubes, both sitting up and looking around as confused as Kaia had been not long ago. If nothing else, the four of them had each other to lean on until Aerin filled them in, or Lena arrived. She remembered that their names were Petra – a black haired, brown eyed elf of a woman – and Dania – a blond haired woman whose presence immediately felt larger than life.

Within minutes, Olya was being assisted to her feet and three additional chairs were being added next to the one Kaia had used. She helped Olya over to the one closest to them and took the next nearest. She didn't know the other two women, but they both smiled and nodded their heads as they also sat.

Aerin stood in front of them while her assistant ran scanners over them. "I'm Aerin. I know you all have questions about the Kraken's journey and where you've ended up. Know that you're safe and that others from the ship have been awake and on our planet for several months now."

"How do you expect us to believe that?" Petra, who sat at the far end of the row, looked down at all of them. She ran her fingers through her black curly hair, bringing some of the bounce back to life. "For all we know you could be preparing to sell us off to the highest bidder."

The look of abject horror on Aerin's face was unmistakable. "Neither the Grus, nor the Fallen would do such a thing. Ever."

"Look, if they were going to hurt us, I don't think they'd have taken the time to bring us out of stasis and make sure that we're healthy." Kaia got to her feet to stand in front of Aerin. "Plus, she learned Earth standard somehow. I'm going to believe her until proven otherwise."

Aerin nodded once. "Thank you."

"I'm ready for those nanobots."

Dania, who'd been quiet up to this point straightened. "Whoa, wait. What nanobots?"

"Aerin here is going to inject nanobots into my body. They act as a translation device and help repair any physical damage that we're suffering from." Kaia knew she was taking a chance here with alien tech, but the opportunity for it to help Olya was too great to pass up.

"Kaia, don't be stupid." Olya shifted in her seat, clearly wanting to get up to try and stop her. "Let's wait until Lena gets here before we do anything that you might regret."

"I wish we had the time to wait." Aerin held up the injector for everyone to see. "It would make the next part of this situation make more sense." Without further explanation, she pressed the injector to the side of Kaia's neck.

A cold rush flowed through her veins, sending a chill through Kaia's body. She waited for the pain that Aerin had mentioned, but other than a mild headache and a small wave of nausea, she felt okay. Aerin watched her intently, her face relaxing when Kaia smiled at her. "I think I'm okay."

"Excellent." Aerin nodded toward her assistants who moved toward the others. "I cannot force any of you to accept this injection, but I promise it will benefit you in more ways that you can imagine."

The three women all looked at Kaia, who could only shrug. "I feel fine. And I think I'm actually starting to understand what they're saying." She pointed at two technicians speaking to one another off to the side. "That's...really weird."

Olya looked at Kaia, and she knew exactly what her twin was thinking: is this going to cure me?

Kaia had spent most of her life feeling that she needed to keep her twin safe, to help her live the life that she wanted. There were many times Kaia had taken work shifts posing as Olya so she could rest, even if Olya hadn't fought against the idea. While it drove Olya nuts, they both wanted her to get better which meant she needed as much rest as possible.

Did Kaia have a bit of a martyr complex? Probably.

But she'd do anything for her sister.

Olya let out a long slow breath before finally nodding. "Let's do this."

Both Petra and Dania also agreed.

"Thank you. Not only will this ensure you don't infect our people with any unexpected illnesses, but it will also help with communication with people other than myself and the doctor." Aerin visibly tensed. "I do have additional information that needs to be shared with you. Based on how some of the other humans have responded, I'm not certain how you'll feel."

Olya cocked her head to the side and frowned the way only her sister did. It was the way her mother always told them apart. "I seriously don't know if I should be scared by that proclamation or not."

"I'm not exactly excited." Petra crossed her arms as she leaned back against her seat. "Why don't you tell us, and we'll do our best not to overreact."

"Yeah, I don't think I'll make that promise." Dania chuckled. "I have a bad habit of overreacting."

Aerin gave Dania a look that Kaia couldn't quite place. "Thank you for your honesty."

Did aliens do sarcasm? Apparently.

Aerin held the injector up and began to press it against Olya's neck. "If it's okay with you, I'd like to complete the injections before I relay the next part. It's better to complete one task before beginning another."

"Do both. I think I'd prefer if you did both." Petra bent her head so Aerin had clear access.

"As you wish." Aerin's expression never changed, but Kaia couldn't help but feel the cyborg was pondering exactly how to tell them…whatever it was she was concerned about. "It is my understanding that all of you boarded the Kraken for different reasons. But according to Lena, Carys, and the others I've spoken to, you all were drawn to the ship. You were all fixated on a certain place in the sky that you knew in your heart you wanted to visit."

Olya sat up straighter. "How did you know that?"

"Wait." Kaia turned to her sister. "You never told me you were fixated on the sky." To be honest, she hadn't said anything to Olya about her own longing to escape Earth's surface and disappear into the inky darkness either.

"You never asked." Olya held her gaze and Kaia felt as though she'd somehow screwed up.

"The sector of space you were all fixated with was ours, and the ultimate destination of the Kraken." Aerin moved down the line to stop in front of Dania. "The reason is you all apparently have an…intimate connection with some of our men. You are their destined mates."

Kaia's eyes widened, as Aerin's words sunk in. "Pardon? You didn't mention anything about a mate. I didn't jump into a transport ship to end up getting partnered off to an alien."

And yet, the panic or anger she would have assumed would accompany such a declaration didn't materialize. There was a small part of her, a dark corner in the back of her brain that knew what Aerin said was the truth. She might have gotten on the Kraken to help Olya, but there'd been another reason, one that she'd refused to acknowledge before now.

There was something…someone here for her. Based on the confused looks on the faces of the other women, they knew it too.

"I understand that this isn't anything that you planned for." Aerin sighed as she pressed the final injection into Dania's neck before stepping back to look at them all. "I would like to be able to tell you the details, that we've determined how and why this connection between the women on the Kraken and some of our cyborg men occurred in the first place. However, we haven't yet been able to determine the how and why this connection has formed."

"Is Lena aware of what's happened here?" Petra leaned forward, resting her forearms on her knees. "That injection packs a bit more punch than I'd expected."

"The discomfort will pass." Aerin set the injector on a table to the side. "Yes, Lena is aware. It was her arrival that made our people…that awakened her mate to her presence."

Kaia shared a look with the others, asking the question they all no doubt had. "Where's she now?"

Aerin cocked her head to the side and an assistant scurried over to her with a data pad in hand. "She couldn't be here, but maybe this will help ease your concerns."

Pressing a few buttons, Aerin turned the data pad around to show Lena's smiling face. "Hey! I'm sorry I couldn't be there like I promised."

"Lena." Dania shifted to the edge of her seat. "How's the weather?"

That was a strange question to ask given their circumstances. But before Kaia could say anything, Lena was chuckling. "Sunny, warm and clear skies."

Dania nodded and sat back against her seat. "That's good to hear."

Lena shrugged. "We'd setup a code just in case there was a problem on arrival."

"I'm the paranoid type." Dania smirked.

"Something I'm now appreciative of." Lena looked at someone off screen. "I wish I could be there to greet you all in person, but I've been trying to establish a neighborhood of sorts for us to move into. I'll leave you in Aerin's capable hands and I'll see you all soon. Man, do I have some stories to tell you."

Dania looked at the others. "That's okay, I know I appreciate having at least this call."

"I do as well." Kaia wished she'd had the presence of mind back on Earth to have setup a code word the way Dania had. "When will we get to see you?"

Lena shrugged, and Kaia noticed how tired the captain looked. "I'm not sure. Rykal and I have been working hard to get everything ready. I just…if you can do everything they ask you to, that would mean a lot."

"How long have we been in stasis?" Olya's quiet voice sent a shiver through Kaia. She hadn't even considered asking that.

"It's been about fifty years."

That piece of information hit Kaia like a punch to the chest. "That's...wow."

"Wait," Petra shifted closer to the screen, "what about these mates Aerin mentioned? Is that real?"

Lena's gaze flicked once more to a spot beyond the screen. "It is. Ah, Aerin, did you tell them about the sex thing?"

"Not yet." Aerin cringed. "I wouldn't have put it quite that way."

Lena's face turned red, even as Kaia and the others openly gaped. "Shit, sorry. It's not as bad as I just made it sound."

"Really?" Petra shook her head. "Cause I don't want to be forced to have sex with a creature I haven't laid eyes on."

"I just woke up after just having been on Earth!" Dania spoke at the same time. "I'm not about to prostitute myself!"

"No, no, no, it's not like that." Lena groaned and rubbed at her eye. "I'm sorry, I'm screwing this up. Aerin can fill you in on the plan, but they won't do anything that you're uncomfortable with. And while I know that makes things complicated for everyone, it will work out for the best. I promise. Okay?"

The four of them nodded, even though Kaia herself still felt uncertain.

"I have to go. Aerin will look after you and I'll see you all soon." The coms channel closed, their four faces reflected back at them in the now black screen.

Petra shook her head. "Not the wake up call I'd been anticipating."

"Where are these supposed mates of ours?" Olya's voice was stronger than it had been a few moments earlier.

"They're waiting for you in one of the upper rooms of the facility." Aerin laced her hands behind her back.

Kaia stood and moved over to her sister, helping her to her feet. "Well, if we have mates, let's go meet them."

CHAPTER FOUR

It was strangely familiar, walking through the plain corridors of a building she knew she'd never been in before now. Maybe that was because all hospitals – even ones on alien worlds – exuded the same feelings that were somehow absorbed by the very structure of the building. The need to help, the pain of injuries, the abundance of grief when all hope was lost; Kaia realized that maybe there were indeed truths that spanned the universe. Love and loss, birth, and death.

With each step they took following Aerin through the facility on their way to meet the four men they were apparently destined to be mated to, Kaia couldn't help but feel as though there was something not quite right with the situation. It wasn't the idea that they were predestined to find their way across space to be with these people, but something else. Something she couldn't put her finger on.

As they made their way, a trio of men who appeared to be soldiers joined them, silently falling into step behind them as they moved. Kaia couldn't imagine they were there to ensure that their group wouldn't cause problems – based on the level of cybernetics that Aerin herself possessed, all four of them wouldn't be able to overpower a single cyborg, let alone need to be subdued by military with blasters – which made her wonder who exactly they were here to protect.

After what felt like a year, they finally stopped in front of a closed door. Aerin turned to face them, that polite smile of hers fixed in place. "Inside are your mates. They've been given an injection to help them keep their baser impulses in check, allowing you the opportunity to meet them, to speak and familiarize yourself with them before more amorous activities proceed."

"I see men are the same no matter where we go."

"It's more than that." Aerin shook her head before letting out a soft sigh. "Actually, it probably isn't."

"Why do I get the impression that you have the patience of a saint, Aerin?" Dania chuckled. "How will we know who our mate is?"

Olya patted Kaia's supporting arm, encouraging her to let go. "I don't know how, but I think it will be painfully obvious as soon as we open that door."

"She's right." Aerin lifted her hand, hovering her finger above the door lock. "Are you ready?"

They all nodded, but Kaia moved to be the first one to enter. Since she'd been the reason the others had agreed to go along with everything in the first place, being the first one in line in case of a problem made the most sense. "Let's do this."

The door hissed open as Aerin stepped aside, leaving Kaia in full sight of the men within. She was vaguely aware of the doctor who'd briefly visited them in the stasis room, along with several other medical staff and cyborgs. She knew they were there, all staring at her, and she also knew that the only one of them who mattered was the man who'd stepped ahead, waiting for her.

His piercing green eyes glowed much the same way that Aerin's did, except the intensity of his gaze felt like a knife into her heart. He was taller than Kaia, muscular, but not as large of frame as the other men in the room. She could see that his left arm was cybernetic, but she didn't know if his body held other cybernetics. No doubt, it was only a matter of time before she'd find out. His black hair was pulled back, his beard graying around the edges. Kaia might not know who he was, his name, where he came from, anything, but she knew in her heart that he belonged to her.

Her mate.

She took a step into the room, aware of Olya's presence behind her, no doubt watching her every move, ready to try and help if something bad were to happen. The man didn't move, but she could tell he was struggling to hold himself still, waiting for her to come to him. When she got close enough to see the fine lines around his eyes, but far enough away that she hoped she was still out of his reach, Kaia stopped. "Hello." Her voice cracked, and she took a moment to clear it. "I'm Kaia."

He sucked in a breath. "I'm Eion."

The sound of his name echoed around her head for a few minutes before she took a chance and smiled at him. "It's nice to meet you."

She took a closer look at the other cyborgs who stood just as still as Eion. They weren't paying her the least bit of attention, their gazes focused on the women behind her. The one with glowing blue eyes was looking at Olya. There was something unnerving at the intensity of all their demeanours focused on the humans. It was as though they'd kill, die, do anything to keep Kaia and the others safe.

"I knew you were coming." The gravelly tone of Eion's voice sent another small shiver through her. "The moment before that door opened, I knew it would be you standing there."

"I..." What the hell could she possibly say to that? "I don't even know what I'm doing yet, how could you?"

She'd half expected him to shrug, but instead he simply stared at her.

The invisible pull between them was stronger than Kaia would have assumed for having just met him. She took another step forward, no longer worried about the others, only wanting to know what it would be like to have Eion wrap his arms around her. She shouldn't care and yet in that moment it was the single most important thing to her. As if he'd known what she was thinking, his hand began to lift and drew close to cupping her cheek.

A moment before his cybernetic hand touched her face, a loud shout followed by an explosion and scream ripped through the room. The force of the blast sent Kaia sprawling, her head connecting with a hard snap against the cold floor. The ringing in her ears was so loud it nearly drowned out the sound of shouting and blaster fire that had erupted around her.

Shit. What's happening?

She finally got her body to cooperate and rolled onto her stomach, braced to move the second her brain could register what she'd need to do. But the moment she moved a wave of nausea made it next to impossible for her to do anything else. Her vision had blurred, and her body refused to cooperate further, even as a part of her brain was screaming at her to move, get out of the way, find cover so she was safe.

Eion had been pushed back by the blast and she could see he was sprawled off to the side. Someone was firing at all the cyborgs from behind her, keeping them from being able to reach her and the other women.

Olya!

Kaia forced herself to glance behind her, but there was no sight of her sister or the other women amidst the smoke and chaos. Shadows of people moving danced with beams of light as fires flickered in the corridor behind them. Olya was there, she could be hurt or worse. Kaia began to crawl back toward the doorway, determined to find her sister even if her concussed head protested the movement.

"No!" Eion was trying to get to her but was pinned in place by another onslaught of blaster fire. "Stay there!"

Absolutely not.

While Eion supposedly was her mate, Olya was *definitely* her sister, and the one person in the universe that she would do anything for. Kaia continued to crawl, even as the smoke clawed at her lungs and brought tears to her eyes the deeper she moved into the chaos around her. "Olya!" Sucking in a lung full of smoke, she coughed so hard she nearly vomited. "Olya!"

The sound of her sister's scream was far away, but distinguishable. "Kaia!"

She was about to shout again, when a hand shot out of the smoke and grabbed her wrist, trying to pull her forward. Kaia jerked backward, trying to break herself free, a scream ripping from her as she struggled. "Let me go!"

Fingers dug into her forearm, sending pain shooting up her arm. Her head was too wonky for her to think straight and all she could do was let her instincts and self-preservation take over. She might not be strong enough to pull free, but she'd be dammed if she'd make it easy for them. Flailing, she pulled, rolled, kicked, and screamed as hard as she could, doing anything to try and loosen their grip on her. For the briefest of moments, she thought there was no way she'd be okay, which was fine if she were with Olya once more.

Then she heard the growl.

Time seemed to slow as her gaze immediately snapped to Eion. He was racing toward her, mouth open, shouting so loud it overpowered everything else. The grip on her arm relaxed for a moment before her assailant yanked her once more, far harder than before, and pulled her fully into the smoke, blinding her.

This is it, I'm dead.

She'd come all the way out into the darkness of space, to end up on an alien planet, only to get kidnapped by someone who probably wanted to sell her off into slavery or to be used as food.

It was exactly the kind of luck that had chased her most of her life, and god she was really getting sick of living this way. For once she'd like to have something be easy, to go her way without the entire universe working against her.

The growl she'd heard from Eion morphed into a scream of rage that penetrated through the madness and echoed through her body. The alien tightened his grip and yanked Kaia once again, so he now hovered over her. His face was covered with a mask, the black material reflecting a distorted image of her face back at her. She didn't like the tired and scared woman she saw, and quickly smiled up at him.

"He's pissed off now." She couldn't help but laugh, not fully understanding why she knew the fool who was trying to pull her away was about to regret that decision.

"Shut up." He grabbed her by the throat, nearly cutting off her oxygen. "Move."

Kaia was yanked to her feet and tossed around as though she weighed nothing. Maybe to him she didn't. She couldn't pull in enough air, her head throbbed and for a moment she though she was going to die. All it would take would be for him to squeeze a tiny bit too hard and her throat would be crushed. She clawed at his hand but couldn't find a grip as panic filled her.

He forced her forward, sending her stumbling a single step before his body was jerked to the side. He didn't release his grip on her shoulder fast enough before he was sent flying through the air, his fingers slicing through the thin fabric of her shirt, leaving deep gouges in her skin and muscles. Kaia screamed, falling to the floor in a heap, only able to watch as Eion tore her would-be kidnapper apart.

Literally apart.

Bile flooded her mouth and for a moment she thought she would vomit, but before that could happen a wave of dizziness slammed into her, making it impossible to keep upright. Collapsing to the floor, she closed her eyes and tried to breathe through the intense pain and panic that threatened to overwhelm her mind. She had to keep moving, had to do everything in her power to not give up.

They had Olya. She needed to pull herself together so she could save Olya.

Kaia sucked in a breath, but even that simple motion sent unbearable pain through her body. Closing her eyes, she tried to mentally accept the pain, to let it wash through her so she could move beyond it. "Shit." This was too much. Everything that had happened over the past day – half century – was simply too much.

No.

Come on, asshole, pull yourself together.

Your sister needs you.

Her head swam and even blinking did little to clear her vision. All Kaia could see was Eion pummeling her attacker before standing up and turning to face her. His hands were covered in blood and the look on his face was nothing less than primal. That was the last thought that passed through her head before she let go and descended into darkness.

CHAPTER FIVE

Eion had never been blinded by rage until this moment. Watching as Kaia was pulled into the smoke, feeling her fear and pain as though it was his own, caused something deep inside him to snap. She was his, and he'd *fraking* destroy anyone who hurt her.

"Eion, no!" Hallam's voice echoed around him, but there was no way he'd listen.

Stepping out into the line of blaster fire, he dodged and rolled for cover, knowing he didn't have much time to free Kaia from her kidnapper. The first shot that connected with his shoulder, sent him stumbling backward, the surge of blaster energy threatening to overwhelm his cybernetics. They'd clearly prepared with weapons designed to incapacitate cyborgs, meaning they knew exactly what they were doing and who they were going against.

The injection Hallam had given him to help ease the mating urges with Kaia were also blocking their cybernetic link, making it difficult to coordinate with the others. He had to believe that they'd understand what he was doing and follow suit without him needing to speak. Eion looked over at Gadiel, whose attention was also split, no doubt worried about his own mate. When they finally made eye contact, Eion cocked an eyebrow and nodded once more toward the doorway where he knew the women were being loaded onto a transport shuttle. They were quickly running out of time to save them and had to act now.

Gadiel was never a man to hesitate, shouting at the others who were pinned down by blaster fire. They'd move as one unit, overwhelm the attackers, and get their mates back safely. It would only take a moment –

Panic.

Kaia couldn't breathe, pain filled her body and she thought she was going to die. Eion didn't know how he knew this, but he did. There was no time to wait, to coordinate, to tell the others. She needed him.

Now.

Rage fueled him as he got to his feet and let out a cry of anguish he didn't know he possessed. Blaster fire connected with his chest and thigh, but Eion felt nothing. Everything in his entire being was focused on Kaia and her pain. Stepping through the smoke, he switched his vision to infrared and was quickly able to locate her. She was being yanked by her throat and he felt her emotions churn as she knew she was about to die.

All rational thoughts fled his mind. Eion lunged at her attacker as he shifted his hold on her, yanking his body away from her with a single motion, sending him flying against a wall. Her pain sliced through him as though it were inflicted on his person. Grabbing the attacker, Eion pulled at him, screaming as a madness descended upon him. He couldn't see, couldn't think, driven only by insanity and the urge to protect. Even when he was pulled off the remnants of the body he'd been punching, Eion wasn't able to snap free of the bloodlust he'd fallen under. It wasn't until someone injected him with something else that slowly the rage receded, and he was once again able to breathe.

"Kaia?" He swallowed past the tightness of his throat, his gaze frantically looking for her. "Where is she?"

"Someone grab a medical unit. Now!" Hallam's voice echoed over the sound of Weixler and Qwin's shouts. "Hurry!"

It was then that Eion was able to focus on who Hallam was leaning over – Kaia's prone and unmoving body. "No."

He tried to pull forward, but Gadiel's grip tightened. "Give them space to work."

"She needs me."

"She needs a doctor. Don't *fraking* move." He tightened his grip on Eion's shoulder as though to reinforce his statement.

"What happened? I don't…I can't remember."

Gadiel sighed but didn't answer. All Eion could do was stand there and watch as the doctors pressed dressings to a deep wound on her shoulder and inject another batch of nanobots into her body. He knew they were communicating through the link, but Eion was still unable to hear them. Not knowing what was happening was almost too much for him to handle.

Finally, Hallam seemed to relax and glanced over their way. "He can come over."

Eion was moving before Gadiel completely let go. "Is she going to be okay?"

"The wound is deep, but I think the nanobots were able to stabilize her. We'll have to wait and see." Hallam sat back on his heels, closed his eyes for a moment as he let out a sigh. "Do we know what happened to the others?"

Gadiel stepped beside Eion. "Aerin was injured but she appears to be functional. Our mates…they're gone."

It was only then that Eion realized Weixler and Qwin were nowhere in sight. Looking around what was left of the corridor, he spotted them standing outside in the swirling wind firing blasters into the sky. The others, their mates, had been taken by the attackers. Only Kaia had been saved, and there was still a chance that she might not survive. Eion dropped to his knees so he could brush Kaia's long brown hair from her face. "We need to go after them."

Hallam glanced over at Aerin who was busy helping the other Fallen who'd been injured in the attack. "I've reached out to the computer to send a distress call to Rykal. He'll notify the Grus and we should be able to track the shuttle of whoever took them. It won't take long."

As Eion sat there staring at Kaia, the strangest feelings slowly washed over him. Part of him was still blindingly furious at the audacity of the attack on their mates, but there was a quieter part that was relieved that his mate hadn't been taken. She might be injured, the nature of her recovery still questionable, but she was here with him. He could reach out and kiss her parted lips, pull her to his chest and listen to her heartbeat. None of the others had that.

He'd never felt so selfishly relieved.

The injection that Hallam had given them all earlier was starting to wear off. With each passing moment Eion felt her emotional and physical presence stronger than the last. As she crept closer to total consciousness, she became confused, scared, angry but not at him or the other Fallen. The pain in her shoulder was intense, but he was surprised at how well she simply accepted the pain and did her best to move through it without becoming overwhelmed. That was the sort of response he'd expect from a Fallen, maybe some of the Grus soldiers, but not an alien race.

He shouldn't be surprised. Someone who was destined to be his mate would need to be strong-willed if they were going to have any chance at being with him.

Without waiting for Hallam's approval, Eion scooped Kaia up, cradling her to his chest as gently as he could manage and stood. "I'm taking her."

"You're doing no such thing." Hallam was on his feet in front of him far faster than he would have guessed the doctor could have moved.

"I'm not leaving her here. I'm taking her someplace safe, somewhere I can protect her."

A muscle in Hallam's jaw jumped as his gaze flicked between Eion and Kaia. Eion didn't need to be connected through the cybernetic link to know what Hallam was thinking. He had a mate of his own, and if his connection to her was even a fraction of what Eion was feeling toward Kaia, then Hallam also knew there was no point in arguing.

"Take her to the East wing, second floor. There are secure rooms where you can keep her safe. I will be checking in with my patient to ensure she's healing properly." Hallam might be a man of peace and healing, but he was also protective of those under his care. This was the best option that would appease them both.

Eion turned and left for the rooms, not able to stop and tell Gadiel or the others what he was doing. No doubt, Hallam would fill them in. The only thing that mattered to him was Kaia and keeping her safe. Ignoring the looks passers by gave him, he made his way as quickly as he could manage without jostling her too much. With each step he could feel the grasp he had on his control begin to slip, the anger and possessiveness battling within him. His desire to claim Kaia for his own so no other would dare touch her again becoming intense. It was only a short matter of time before the injection would be out of his system and he wasn't certain he'd be able to control himself.

He needed her.

Needed to mark her as his own. Needed to feel her body accept his cock as she writhed beneath him. Eion had never felt this way toward another being, never wanted to give himself over so completely. Even his connection with the others – Gadiel, Weixler and Qwin – he'd always held a small part of himself back, as though he'd known he needed to keep it for someone else.

Now he knew it belonged to Kaia.

It didn't take him long to find an empty room where Hallam

had indicated, giving him a small sense of relief as he walked in, locked the door, and placed her gently on the bed. Straightening, he stared down at her, doing his best to come to terms with his growing awareness of her emotions. He knew the nanobots were doing their best, working quickly to heal her wounds so she could wake once again. As much as the urge to touch her was powerful, he knew he needed to give her time.

Grabbing a chair, he pulled it over to the side of the bed and sat down, bracing his forearms on his thighs. He'd keep watch over her until he knew she was out of danger.

Then he'd make her his.

KAIA COULDN'T OPEN her eyes, but she knew she was being watched. She felt the weight of a stare on her, could smell his sweat as heat from his body rolled across her arm. She didn't know how long she'd been sleeping, didn't know where she was, but with absolute certainty, she knew that Eion was here with her, keeping watch.

Keeping her safe.

This should be creepy, shouldn't it? Having a stranger sit with her in a room watching her? Even though she'd done essentially the same thing with Olya over the years, especially on the days when her Breneman's virus flared up, pushing her sister into hours of full body pain, night terrors, and hallucinations.

Her mind was fully awake, though she was still unable to move her body. Kaia tried to picture Eion, remember the intensity of his glowing eyes as her instant attraction confused her as much as it enticed. She'd been attracted to men over the years, but she rarely had taken the time to date. Working and helping to care for her twin had comprised most of her life, and wanting to spend time with a man was, well, far too selfish.

The pain in her shoulder had lessened, so she was able to shift and stretch on the bed she realized she'd been placed on. With her eyes still closed, she could almost picture Eion sitting there, cataloguing her every move, almost hear his internal monologue. Wondering if she was still hurt, if he'd be able to touch her soon, be able to kiss her.

Kaia's eyes flew open at that, and her gaze was immediately captured by his.

"You want to kiss me?" She hadn't meant to ask the question, but she also didn't think she'd have been able to stop herself.

The muscles in his throat tightened as he swallowed, and the light in his eyes flared bright. "Yes."

She understood his alien words as though he'd spoken in Earth standard, which she assumed meant the nanobots that Aerin had injected into her were doing what they were supposed to. "Did you find the others? Were you able to get my sister back?"

"Not yet. We're tracking the shuttle. It's only a matter of time." His gaze flicked across her face, down her body, and back up to her shoulder. She could feel his assessment of her physical state with the weight of his stare. "You're still healing."

She was, but Kaia wasn't exactly someone who let physical pain hold her back. She ignored his noise of protest as she gingerly sat up. "I'm fine. I need to find my sister."

"Gadiel and the others are already looking. They won't stop until they know their mates are safely back with them."

Even if Aerin hadn't told her that Eion and the others were their supposed mates, Kaia would have known there was something special between her and Eion. A spark that sent a tremor through her body, making her painfully aware of the caress of his breath against her skin and his body heat against her. The thought that Olya might have a similar connection with one of the other aliens, well, she hadn't mentally wrapped her head around that yet.

She hadn't fully wrapped her head around Eion either.

It took effort not to notice that he was little more than a solid wall of muscle and cybernetics, and despite the similarities between their people and humans, she would have known they weren't the same species. The whole uncanny valley feel had her blinking several times and unable to put her finger exactly on what was different. His eyes glowed green and he had visible cybernetics that went from his left hand all the way up, disappearing beneath his shirt. His skin had a slightly green tint to it, making his pulled back hair and bushy beard look at once both human and alien.

In the end, the differences didn't matter, even if she would have like to have known why she was equally attracted to and confused by the intensity of his gaze.

Not that she had time for anything remotely close to a relationship, not when Olya was missing.

Taking a breath, she tried to stand but was immediately stopped by Eion's large hands on her arms. "No."

"What do you mean *no*? If people are looking for my sister and the others, then I'm damn well going to be there to help."

"You're in no physical condition to help anyone. You need to rest and let the nanobots finish their job." He could have easily forced her back onto the bed, but he simply stared at her with those glowing green eyes of his, until she felt guilty for trying to argue. "They'll find her."

"I realize you don't know me or the type of person I am, but I'm not going to sit on the sidelines while aliens rush off to find my sister. She's the single most important person to me in the entire galaxy and I'm not going to be able to rest while I know that she's in danger."

Eion dropped his hold on her arms and cocked his head to the side. "More important than I am?"

"Sorry to burst your bubble, but we've only just met."

"I'm your mate. Your life partner."

"Yes, I've been told that more than once now." Kaia let out a huff. "But she's my twin. We've never been apart like this before and I'll be damned if I sit here and not do everything in my power to get her back. As my mate, you can either help me or get out of my way."

It probably wasn't the smartest move to antagonize an alien soldier who'd torn an enemy literally apart, but she was truly beyond caring. If he was actually the man she was supposed to spend the rest of her life with, then he better damn well get used to her. Based on the look he was currently giving her, he might be regretting the entire thing.

"Well, are you going to take me to the others so I can help find my sister?" The pain in her shoulder was already lessening, so hopefully by the time she was able to do something she'd be physically up for it.

"I will under one condition."

"What's that?"

Eion cocked an eyebrow as he narrowed his gaze. "Prove to me that you're physically able to handle the strain."

Kaia wasn't used to being the one who was challenged, often being on the other side of that equation. But if he wanted her to prove that she was feeling okay, then fuck it, that's what she'd do.

Leaning in, she took his face in her hands and kissed him.

Hard.

CHAPTER SIX

Eion knew she was going to kiss him seconds before she did, and he still wasn't prepared for the rush of intense possessiveness he felt from the first brush of her lips against his. The injection that Hallam had given him was wearing off, making each passing moment more difficult for him to keep hold of his control. Especially as Kaia slid a hand from his face, down the side of his neck to cup the base of his head. The touch was intimate and felt as possessive of him as he was of her.

And he'd only known of her existence for a few hours.

Kaia let her tongue brush against his, the soft heat brought his cock to life and a rush of blood to his *rondella*, the male sex organ on the inside of his thigh that hadn't shown signs of life since his rebirth. Startled, he pulled back and sucked in a sharp breath, trying to regain a small measure of the composure he so desperately needed.

"What?" Kaia's lips were parted, wet, plump from the hard contact they'd just shared.

He wished she were able to feel his emotional state the way he apparently could hers. It would save him struggling for words that he wouldn't have been good at finding even before he'd been reborn. Eion had always been a man of acts rather than words, and the one act he wanted more than anything to do with Kaia was one that would cause her more harm than good.

With effort of will and care to not touch her still healing wound, he gently moved her away from him. "You're still hurt."

"I'm well aware." Her smirk and the way she licked her lower lip fired his blood. "You're the one who wanted me to prove that I could physically handle the strain. This is the best way I presently know how."

The temptation was far stronger than it should have been for him. He needed to protect her, to ensure that she'd forever be safe and not have to fear for her life. At least, that's what he'd always assumed a Grus female wanted when looking for a mate. He'd never had much of an opportunity to be with someone long-term before the Sholle war and his subsequent death and rebirth. Eion had enlisted into the Grus military long before any attacks, wanting nothing more than to serve his planet and her people. For him, that meant giving up the thought of having a family of his own. The idea of putting his life in danger knowing that there was someone waiting for him to return never sat well. He couldn't cautiously complete missions that required taking risks to succeed, just to safeguard his own life so he could return to another.

But the war with the Sholle was long over and Eion was all alone.

Well, not really.

Kaia tugged at him and he knew she wanted him to join her on the bed. It was his fault for taunting her into proving that she was feeling well enough physically to go after her sister. He should have realized that the humans would be similar to Grus in that they put their family relations high on their priority chain. He didn't quite understand the significance of what it meant to be a twin, but clearly the status was important to her.

And now she wanted to be intimate with him to prove her ability to care for her sister.

"This isn't right." Momentum kept him moving to sit on the bed beside her, but he didn't allow her to push him any further. "You don't need to do this."

His body screamed at him that yes, she really did need to do this and so did he. It had been over fifty years since he'd been intimate with anyone, since the day before his death and rebirth. Kaia's touch ignited a part of him he'd long thought dead, and it wasn't entirely physical.

The growl that left his body was so primal it startled even him as he moved forward until she was lying flat on the bed. The surge of desire, the urge to press her into the bed while licking and kissing every inch of her body was so strong, he had to close his eyes and force himself to hold back, even if it was for only a moment. He couldn't do anything to hurt her, couldn't take the chance that he'd ruin this thing between them before he'd even had the opportunity to see what it was. She might be his mate, but that didn't mean he didn't owe her respect, time to adjust to her new world and circumstances.

"Breathe." Kaia's voice somehow penetrated his brain fog, making him aware of her fingers sliding back and forth across his chest. "Just breathe."

"I don't understand…" He closed his eyes and sucked in a breath. "Why I'm responding this way."

"I can't pretend to even guess but the others seemed to know that this would happen. I know things will ease for you if we have sex. Let's have sex and then we can figure everything else out after that."

Any remaining ability to hold himself back was gone as her words blasted through the last of his resolve. Lowering his mouth to hers, his matrix stored every detail about her that he could manage. The way she sighed as he swiped his tongue across hers, the flex of her arms around his shoulders, the press of her nails into the fabric of his uniform. When he pressed his hard cock against the apex between her thighs, he reveled in the moan that slipped from her and the way she moved hard against him.

If this was nothing more than an act, she was a master performer.

She began to pull at his clothing as he continued to kiss and nip at her, running his tongue down the side of her throat, careful to avoid her injured shoulder. He could see the nanobots were busy at work repairing the damage, but he didn't want to delay her healing simply because he wanted to mark her as his own. Instead, he helped her remove his uniform, kicking his boots to the floor while breaking physical contact with her for as short a time as possible.

The cold air of the room helped to ease his burning desire enough for him to set to work removing her clothing. With each inch of newly revealed skin, Eion's desire deepened for this alien woman who'd somehow arrived when he didn't know he needed someone. Her skin was lighter than the Grus, but not as light as some of the other humans he'd seen. She was perfect, soft, round in all the places that appealed to him sexually, but with an unmistakable physical and mental strength that he sensed drove her forward.

Her breasts were large, easily filling most of his palm when he cupped her, squeezing her hard enough to pull a gasp. Her pupils had grown wide, swallowing up most of the brown that he'd already grown accustomed to seeing in the short time they'd known one another. "You enjoy that."

"I do." Her tongue darted out to lick her bottom lip.

Eion didn't need her to speak for him to be aware of her rising desire, to know that she wanted him to pinch the darkened nipples between his fingers, that she wanted to reach between her thighs and stroke the sensitive part between them, needed to feel pleasure even if there was a part of her that felt guilty for desiring him.

Her sister was still missing, in danger, and here she was enjoying herself.

Kaia stiffened and withdrew slightly. "I need to find Olya."

"We will. The others are already looking for her, I promise you. They'll stop at nothing to get their mates back. They'll punish those who took them." Rage at the mere thought of someone touching, let alone taking Kaia from him, coursed through Eion. "We can stop if you want. I'll never force you."

Her indecision flashed once more, but as before he felt her quash it. "No. I want this. And knowing Olya, she'd get pissed if she thought I didn't think she could handle herself."

There was something else hidden in her words, but Eion didn't want to take the time to decipher it in the moment. Especially when Kaia reached down and cupped his erect cock and balls in her hand.

"It's surprising that you're physically so similar to humans."

It was Eion's turn to gasp. "I do believe we have some differences. I don't see a *rondollo* on your inner thigh."

"A what?"

He spread his legs and moved her hand so she could touch his. "It's called a *rondella* on a male. An additional step in our reproductive system. You don't seem to have one."

"Will that change anything?" Her fingers continued to trace a pattern across the top of the thin membrane, sending increasing waves of desire through his body until he was vibrating from want.

"If you keep doing that, I won't be able to hold myself back."

Kaia smiled, her tongue darting out once more. "That doesn't sound like a bad thing."

"You might live to regret those words."

She gently squeezed his *rondella*, and his body jerked forward, pressing her back hard against the bed. Eion hadn't realized the strength of his reaction until he realized that the tip of his cock was pressed against the opening to her body. It would take nothing for him to push forward and fill her, to finally claim her as his, to make her his own. Looking into her eyes, he could see that she wanted this as badly as he did, leaving nothing in his way to keep him from doing what he wanted.

And yet, there was something holding him back.

His body shook as he appeared unable to move forward. He wanted to feel her around him, know that she was his and would remain forever so. Maybe it was the injection that Hallam had given him, but there was something preventing him from doing what he wanted, from giving in to these base desires that he hadn't felt in over half a century. It wasn't until Kaia cupped his cheek and leaned up to place a soft kiss to his lips that he realized he'd been waiting for her to mentally accept that she did want this as well.

The moment her mouth touched his, he thrust forward, filling her to the hilt. Their gasps were mutual, and in that instant, he realized that his ability to feel her physical responses were heightened by their sexual connection. He became aware of not only where she wanted to be touched, but of the extent of pain she felt in her shoulder. She ignored it, so she could focus on the rush of pleasure spreading through her lower body.

Eion began to thrust into her, a steady rhythm that wouldn't take long for either of them to reach climax. Kaia's eyes were wide, her lips parted as she moaned and bucked against him. He wanted nothing more than to have her reach down and touch his *rondella* again, but given how close he was to release it was probably for the best that she couldn't. He needed to hold back long enough to see her face when she reached her peak. Would her face flush darker than it was now? Would her eyes be opened or closed? It was exciting, erotic not knowing, experiencing something for the first time.

He'd never felt this close, connected to another person before. He wanted to cherish every thought and feeling of hers that brushed across his mind, wanted to worship every patch of her skin. If this was what it meant to have a mate, Eion wanted to drown in the sensation.

What he hadn't anticipated was the sudden urge to mark her as his own, to lean and bite down on her shoulder so no other would go near her. The rush of his own pre-orgasm slammed into him, catching Eion by surprise and ripping a shout from him.

"You okay?" Kaia's fingers dug into his arms even as she continued to grind against him.

"Yes." The word came out more as a hiss. He lowered his forehead to her unhurt shoulder, his lips pressed against her skin.

"I'm...close." Her breath tickled his ear, her soft gasps sending his synapses misfiring.

At the first squeeze of her inner muscles around his cock, Eion rushed headfirst into his release. He let out a shout that swallowed up Kaia's. The crushing force of his orgasm blinded him to everything beyond the smell and feel of her body against him. Without realizing what he was doing, Eion bit down on her shoulder, causing Kaia's body to stiffen with surprise before he regained his control.

They rode through the end of their release until they both stopped moving. Lying together, bodies slick with sweat, panting and clinging to one another. Eion slid to the side, not wanting to crush Kaia under his weight. "Did I harm you?"

"Well, you bit me. But," she looked awkwardly down at her shoulder, "I think I'm okay. You caught me off guard."

Not that he'd admit it out loud, but he'd scared himself. The thought of losing control and harming her turned his stomach. "I believe Hallam's injection allowed me to stop myself from doing too much damage."

"I think I've proven I'm able to handle things, and I would love to stay and cuddle. But ... Olya. I feel so helpless – I need to *do* something, to try and find her." She sat up and crossed her arms, her gaze not meeting his. "She's been the most important person to me my whole life. Knowing that she's out there, that someone could be hurting her as we speak. I can't sit here and put my desires first any longer. I just can't."

Eion felt as though someone had shoved a charged electrode into his matrix. She'd been up front about why she'd agreed to have sex with him, and now she wanted him to uphold his end of the deal. Perhaps she didn't feel the strength of their connection the way he did?

Pushing up from the bed, he kept his back to her as he gathered his clothing. "Yes. Get dressed and I'll inform Gadiel that you'll be coming with us."

"Eion, I – "

"I'll give you privacy to dress." Ignoring the rush of guilt he felt from her, he left the room.

Never again would he make the mistake of letting his heart be vulnerable.

CHAPTER SEVEN

Kaia knew she'd fucked up the moment Eion stood up and left the room. She hadn't intended to hurt him, only prove that she was more than capable physically to help find Olya. Still, mate or not, she wasn't about to let someone she'd just met stand in her way and stop her from ensuring her sister's safety.

Screw that.

She got the impression that Eion and the others were resilient and that he'd survive this little setback between them. It was strange that she was aware of his emotional state, could feel his frustration and disappointment. Her bond with Olya was similar in many ways, though there wasn't an actual mental connection linking them. No matter what was happening, Kaia knew her sister would be analyzing her situation, doing what she could to find a way to freedom. And she wasn't alone, which gave Kaia a small measure of relief.

Being careful not to do more harm to her wounds, Kaia slowly pushed herself up from the bed and got dressed. Despite Eion having left her alone in the room, she could feel that he wasn't too far away. He needed to learn that she was more than capable of looking after herself, that she was the one others came to when a problem needed to be solved. She didn't need him running after her ensuring she didn't stub a toe or get a papercut.

Did they even have paper here?

The nanobots were working hard to fix her up to the point where Kaia felt as though she weren't going to faint, even if her body was still sore from the impact it had absorbed. There didn't appear to be any mirrors in the room she could use to make sure her appearance wasn't horrific, so all she could do was run her hands through her hair, trying to get any knots out. Pulling her hand back she was startled to see her fingers tinged with red. Blood was her enemy, making her woozy whenever she saw it. Why she hadn't immediately passed out when Eion had torn her attacker apart, she wasn't certain.

Shock, no doubt.

There wasn't time for her to have a shower, or even stand here while her thoughts tried to make sense of everything that had happened to her in the short time since she'd been woken from stasis. First thing she needed to do was meet up with the others and learn if they'd figured out where Olya and the others were. Only once she knew that would she worry about getting cleaned up.

Or fixing the hurt she'd caused Eion.

She was aware of his presence in the corridor before the door slid open. He stood leaning against the wall at the other end, close to the elevator they'd come up in. From this distance, his profile made her think of the few nights back on Earth she'd let Olya convince her to go out for an evening and find a club or bar to visit in search of some company. Eion standing like that, his long brown hair pulled into a bun, his beard thick and practically begging her to run her fingers through it, well, she would have been attracted to him immediately. Her body was still tender from their recent bout of sex, a reminder that perhaps some things were still the same no matter where she ended up.

He didn't look at her as she slowly made her way down the hall toward him and the elevator. It was easy to see that his body was taut with tension and the slightest indication that she needed his assistance, he'd snap and race to her side. Kaia ensured she moved slowly enough so that she wouldn't need help, leaving him standing there. It was only when she finally reached his side that he looked up. "The neural blockers Hallam injected into my matrix are mostly worn off now. I'm able to communicate with the others through our link. But not for long. Hallam will be injecting them again momentarily."

Kaia nodded, grateful that her earlier assumption of a link between the others existed. "Have they made any progress?"

"Yes. They'll wait for us to join them before they relay the information."

Kaia might not have known Eion longer than a few hours, but that didn't mean she wanted to see him hurt by her actions. As the door to the elevator slid open and he pushed away from the wall, she put her hand on his shoulder and gave him a soft squeeze. "I'm sorry."

The muscle in his jaw jumped. "As am I. You were honest regarding your actions and intentions. I can't expect you to simply accept what I want as more important, even if I am your mate."

"That's…" Kaia shook her head and chuckled. "You're far more enlightened than a shit-ton of the men back on Earth."

She was only slightly hurt when he stepped away from her touch and into the elevator. "We need to meet with the others in person. Hallam just told me that he's given the others another dosage of the blockers. I can't communicate with them any longer."

"The four of you are close?" Heat from his body warmed her bare arm.

"We're soldiers. Part of a covert unit called the Qadrus. We used to…do the things others did not want to." Eion turned his face slightly so the green glow from his eyes cast deep shadows on his cheeks. "We're closer than brothers."

Perhaps it wasn't so unusual that both she and Olya would find that they were mated to two members of a group as close knit as these four appeared to be.

The short ride down in the elevator did little to ease the rising tension building inside her. She believed that even if they knew exactly where the others were, there was little chance that recovering the other women would go as smoothly as she wanted. She could only hope that the nanobots were doing what they needed to heal Olya. Eion's hand brushed the back of hers, causing her to look up into his eyes.

"She'll be okay. We'll get her back and the two of you can figure out what it means to live here."

"Thanks. I hope you're right."

"I am." He said it with such certainty she nearly believed him.

She could hear loud voices the moment the elevator door slid open. The shouting was tinged with rage and fear, though she wasn't certain who exactly was speaking. Eion strode ahead of her, clearly knowing that his presence was needed to help contain whatever was happening in the room down the corridor.

"Why aren't we on a ship right now? It would take nothing to track them down, retrieve our mates, and blast those *frakers* into space." It was the man with the purple eyes and cybernetics that took up a portion of the side of his neck, shouting and waving his hands around at the others. "This is ridiculous!"

"Calm down, Wex." Eion spoke as they entered the room, causing all eyes to snap to them.

Kaia hadn't felt as though she'd been shoved beneath a microscope before now, but with the intensity of the cyborgs' stares, she knew what it was like. In a rarity for her, a wave of fear and insecurity slammed into her and without thinking, she moved to stand directly behind Eion. She didn't know how, but despite how close he was to the others, she knew in her heart that he'd do anything to defend her and keep her safe.

Weixler snarled at him, bolting toward them. "You shut the *frak* up! Your mate is here safe with you, not ripped from your side by the Black Guard to *frak* knows where."

Eion stiffened. "The Black Guard? They've never attempted to come anywhere near Zarlan or Grus Prime before now. How can you be sure?"

The one with the red eyes took Weixler by the shoulder and yanked him away from where they stood. "Sit down before I let Eion dismantle you piece by piece." He waited for Weixler to do as he was told before holding his hand out toward her. "I'm Gadiel. You've met Weixler, and the other member of our group is Qwin. You're Kaia, yes?"

"I am." Straightening her shoulders, she moved to stand beside Eion. "While I appreciate the pleasantries, I have to say I agree with Weixler here. When are we leaving to get my sister and the others back?"

Gadiel's eyebrow lifted, and he let out a deep chuckle. "She suits you, Eion."

"More to the point, she's not going to sit back and let us find her sister for her. I suggest we come up with a plan now and find your mates before the Guard does something that they'll regret."

"Who are these Black Guard people anyway?" The way that Eion spoke the name, she got the impression they weren't to be trifled with.

"I don't know what your planet or section of the universe is like, but the Black Guard infiltrates planets and sectors, twisting the lives of the inhabitants to a degree that they become completely dependant on the Guard. Then they withhold resources, bleeding the planets dry of their finances and leaving them begging for scraps."

"They sound like the mob back on Earth." She'd come close to needing to deal with them more than a few times over the years, mostly when Olya needed medicine and Kaia wasn't sure where to find it. "If the space mob has my sister then we're damn well going to do everything in our power to get her back. Now."

Weixler grinned. "I like you, human."

"And I'll like you even more when we get the women back safe and sound." At least they were all on the same page regarding the need to mount a rescue. "So, what do we do first?"

Eion followed her as Kaia moved to sit down on the nearest chair. Despite having nanobots working whatever magic they had inside her, she was more than a little exhausted from everything that had happened to her over the past hour or so.

God, she hadn't even been awake a single day and everything had gone to shit. That had to be a new record for the shortest amount of time for a crisis to unfold in her life. Her parents would be furious if they knew Kaia had already let something happen to Olya before she'd even discovered if there was a way to cure her. If her parents were even alive.

Eion's hand landed gently on her shoulder. "What's wrong?"

She hadn't realized that panic and grief were clawing at her chest, making it difficult to breathe. "I just realized that my parents are dead. I just saw them a few hours ago but…that was… they're probably long dead now."

"I'm sorry." There was such kindness and love in his soft whisper of words, the pain in Kaia's chest eased.

Gadiel marched over to a computer terminal. "I've sent a communication to Rykal informing him of what's happened and seeking permission to take a shuttle in pursuit. I stressed that time was of the essence here."

"Who's Rykal?" Kaia whispered once more to Eion.

"The leader of the Fallen, the cyborg people on this planet." His fingers brushed the back of her neck in a soothing rhythm that continued to comfort her. "He also has a human mate, so he'll understand the importance of our request."

"That's good." The more people who were on their side the faster she'd get Olya back.

Qwin pushed away from the wall that he'd been leaning against. "We should have heard back by now. This is a simple recovery mission against a known enemy."

"Agreed." Gadiel frowned down at the computer terminal.

Hallam, who'd been working at a secondary computer, let out a grunt. "Based on these readings, I've made some modifications to the serum. It will increase the length of the dampening effects, and it should be more successful in the management of your aggression and emotional flux regarding your mates. I wasn't able to do anything about the blocking of your use of the cybernetic neural link, so unfortunately you'll all be on your own until this is resolved."

"We've worked together as Grus long before our rebirths." Weixler widened his stance as he crossed his arms. "We'll be fine."

There was a sound from the computer terminal that grabbed everyone's attention. Gadiel pressed a button and the face of another Fallen filled the large screen for everyone to see. Gadiel laced his hands behind his back. "Rykal. We can be on a shuttle and on their trail in a second."

Kaia might not know the man, but even she could tell that what he was about to say wasn't the news they all wanted to hear. His mouth was a thin line and the glow of his crystal blue eyes flared for the briefest of moments.

"You can't go after them."

Kaia mentally blocked out the sounds of the cyborgs yelling, watching blankly as Weixler and Qwin waved their arms at the unmoving Rykal on the screen. Gadiel's hands had fallen to his side, his body tense as though he were about to leap through the screen and murder the man on the other side. Even she wanted nothing more than to scream and cry at the injustice of the situation. Three humans unfamiliar with where they'd landed were snatched away from safety before they'd even had a moment to adjust, and these bastards didn't want to do anything to help?

Fuck them.

It was then that she realized Eion was the only one calm, the only one who didn't react with anger and outrage. And why would he? She was his mate, and she was sitting here safe and sound. Shakily getting to her feet, Kaia turned and glared at him. "Do something."

Eion's demeanor didn't change, but she could tell something inside him shifted. He nodded and walked past her to Rykal. The others fell silent, even Weixler who'd turned to punch a hole in the wall.

"May I ask the reasoning why we're not permitted to retrieve the humans?" Eion laced his hands behind his back much the same way that Gadiel had previously.

"With unification now finalized, we must coordinate with Grus Prime and the high command to ensure we're not creating unnecessary turmoil that will have a negative impact in our re-entry into the political sector of the quadrant. The four of you rushing off to murder half the Black Guard to retrieve three humans will cause more problems than the high command is willing to accept."

When Weixler and Qwin began to protest again, Eion held up his hand to silence them. "This is about politics then. About the need for Grus Prime to maintain their…connections."

"Yes." Rykal lowered his chin, which appeared to make his eyes glow even brighter. "If this was solely my decision to make, I'd already have you on a ship with three others as back up. Even Aidric argued in your favor. But we didn't fight to bring our two people back together just for the first problem we face to tear everything apart. We need to follow the request of the high command and pursue this through proper channels."

"We understand." Eion nodded and immediately ended the

communication before anyone else had an opportunity to say anything.

"What the *frak* do you mean, we understand?" Weixler rushed Eion and grabbed him by the throat. "You don't get to make these decisions for us!"

Eion easily broke Weixler's grip on him and landed a punch that sent the other cyborg to the floor. Kaia gasped and started to go to Eion when he held up his hand. She stopped and could only watch as the men glared at one another.

"Because my mate is here, I'm the only one of us with a mind clear enough to make these decisions. I needed to say what I did to Rykal to give him the benefit of plausible deniability."

Kaia let out the breath she'd been holding. "We're going after them?"

"We're going after them." Eion then grinned in a way that sent a chill through Kaia. "And I promise you this, we're going to make them pay."

CHAPTER EIGHT

Eion didn't need communication through their cybernetic link for the four of them to all know exactly what needed to be done. They'd need a ship, weapons, supplies, and a means of tracking their mates once they were off planet. Hallam might not be a member of their group, but he had the means to give them the tools they needed if they hoped to be successful as quickly as possible. It took Eion giving him a single look for the doctor to leave the room, no doubt in search of whatever injections Gadiel, Weixler, and Qwin would need to keep themselves in control of their emotions.

Though Eion knew there'd be a time and a place for their rage.

Gadiel was by his side, his chin lowered. "Where are you thinking of getting a shuttle?"

"Rykal will be obligated to put the expected resources on lockdown. He'll need to prove to the high command that he'd done everything in his power to prevent our leaving. That leaves the prison defense shuttles, or the mining operation. They have several heavy cruisers we could repurpose."

Zarlan's mines were on the far side of the planet and it would cost them precious time they didn't have getting there. The prison was far closer to the medical facility but had the added challenge of needing to convince Zee, the warden, of the merits of their mission. Zee wasn't exactly known for his easy-going nature, but more for following the letter of Grus and Fallen laws. Running one of the most dangerous prisons in the quadrant of space offered little room for flexibility.

Gadiel let out a soft hum. "Let me reach out to Zee."

It was Eion's turn to snort. "I'll coordinate with Hallam to ensure we have the necessary medical supplies to keep the women healthy."

Kaia had retaken her seat off to the side of the room, but Eion was acutely aware of her emotional turmoil. She shifted from fear that it was already too late to rescue her twin, to anger that this had happened to them, to loneliness. That last emotion Eion didn't understand as he was still here with her. Despite their differences and not fully understanding how this mating bond of theirs worked, there was no denying their connection. She wasn't alone and wouldn't be as long as he lived, even if they didn't share any further intimacies.

"We need weapons." Weixler was hunched over the farthest computer terminal, his purple eyes locked on the screen in front of him. "I've located three of our caches that appear still intact."

"Take a crawler and retrieve them." Gadiel spoke without looking back at him. "Be back as quickly as possible and prepared for departure."

Eion knew he should be assisting the others, but he couldn't help but fixate on Kaia and the torrent of emotions that emanated from her. No longer able to ignore them, he strode over to her, slowing when she looked up at him. He hadn't known a race to be so expressive with their emotions without uttering a single word. Her pain and determination were etched on her face and reflected to him in her gaze.

"We'll get your sister back." Of that he was completely certain.

"The others won't rest until they find their mates. Until they're back with us."

"I know." There was a waver in her voice that betrayed her words.

"You need to trust me. To trust us. The Black Guard had *no* idea who they angered when they took Olya and the others. We'll make them pay for their foolishness."

"I will as well." It was then that she tenderly got to her feet, wincing slightly as she pulled her shoulders back. "I'm going to be with you every step of the way. I'm not going to sit back here waiting for news of Olya's safety. The only reason she's here in the first place is because of me and my idea of finding a cure for her illness. Please don't try and convince me to do otherwise."

Eion could only stare at her, because every word that flipped through his mind was a plea for her to do exactly that. To stay behind and be safe. He'd spent his life avoiding forming relationships with anyone outside of his team for this very reason. None of them could afford to be distracted when out in the field. Knowing she was here waiting for him but safe, was one thing. Having her on the shuttle with them as they went out in search of the Black Guard was something he wasn't prepared to face.

"Gadiel, what the *frak* are you contacting me for?"

Eion turned to see Zee's face fill the communication screen. His cybernetics comprised half his face and made for an intimidating appearance for anyone who wasn't familiar with the warden. Not that Gadiel would be cowed by anyone. "I don't need to ask if you've heard of the attack on the medical facility."

Zee cocked an eyebrow. "I still have the prison on lockdown. Surprised they didn't attempt a breakout."

"No one is that stupid." Gadiel crossed his arms. "The Black Guard took three of our mates."

Something immediately changed in Zee's demeanor as he leaned forward. "Grus Prime won't allow you to go after them?"

"They don't want to destroy diplomatic ties that haven't fully formed."

Eion gave Kaia a glance before joining Gadiel. "You don't seem surprised by our revelation."

"I've been far more engaged in political back channels recently than I care to admit."

That would make their request far easier. Eion and Gadiel shared a brief glance before Gadiel continued. "We need a shuttle to go after them."

"Done. Anything else?"

"That was easy." Gadiel shook his head. "I expected more resistance to our request."

"I would tear the planet apart to get Mags back if someone took her from me." The edge in Zee's voice left no doubt that he spoke the truth.

"Wex and Qwin are gathering the rest of our supplies, and I want to be in space within the hour."

Zee's gaze shifted from Gadiel and Eion to something behind them. Eion turned to see Kaia coming closer to the screen. "I see the Black Guard didn't capture all your mates."

"This is Kaia." Eion wanted to reach for her but kept his arms at his side instead. "Her sister was one of the women they took."

Zee looked at her intently before nodding. "I've seen that same determination on Mag's expression several times now. I have no doubt you'll find your mates and get your sister back safely. Gadiel, you'll need to make it look as though you've stolen the shuttle."

"I wouldn't have it any other way." Gadiel laced his hands behind his back. "Keep your guards at a distance unless you want them injured."

"Their presence is required inside the prison due to the continued lockdown. That will be necessary for at least another several hours. There will only be a few present for appearances."

"Thank you." Gadiel ended communications without another word. "We'll need to move quickly."

"You'll also need a supply of these." Hallam had re-entered the room at some point during the conversation with Zee. He held up a bag briefly before tossing it to Eion. "A supply of the serum and injectors so the three of you are able to maintain your wits. I've also included several doses of additional nanobots and medical supplies in case the women are injured."

"But they've already been given a dose." Kaia stiffened but didn't move. "Will the nanobots you injected into Olya be enough to cure her illness if she's also been hurt?"

"I'm not certain as I haven't had an opportunity to look at her condition in detail. I would recommend another injection once you find her, simply to ensure she's healthy enough to travel. At the very least, if her illness is more extreme than I'd originally surmised, or she's sustained additional damage, then a second dose should be enough to keep her stable until you can return here, and I can run additional scans." Hallam approached Kaia but stopped before he was close enough to touch her. "You'll need to be careful while you're out there as well. Your wounds aren't healed yet and if you push yourself too hard, you'll reinjure yourself."

"She should stay here." The words left Eion before he realized he'd spoken.

Hallam let out a soft sigh. "I know your instincts are to keep your mate safe but having that separation now would be detrimental to you both. Your bond hasn't solidified yet. The chances that you'd lose control while out on mission is great."

"Then I'll take the injection the same as the others." Eion ignored Kaia's open-mouth stare. "I don't want her in harm's way."

Hallam shook his head. "I haven't done any testing on blocking a bond between mates once the process has started. I can't guarantee that will work. Or worse, it will work but it will also cause problems with your bond once it's worn off. Is that a risk you're willing to take?"

Until a short time ago, Eion wasn't aware of Kaia. It shouldn't be a difficult decision for him to make, to ensure she was safe, so he was able to see to his duties.

And yet, even the slightest of chance that something would happen to damage this fledgling relationship wasn't something he could do. "No."

Hallam nodded. "I'll leave you to your preparations." He began to leave but stopped short. "Kaia, might I speak with you for a moment?"

A surge of rage slammed into Eion at the thought of anyone but himself being close to her, and it took considerable effort for him to not lash out at Hallam. All he could do was turn and march away when she let out a soft but firm, "Yes."

If this was what it meant to have a mate, perhaps it was a terrible idea.

Kaia couldn't look at Eion as he left her standing there. She felt his anger and frustration, most of which was directed toward her, and didn't want to deal with him. Instead, she focused her attention on Hallam and the firmness of his green eyes. Other than Zee, he had the most visible amount of cybernetics that she'd seen on any of the Fallen, which should have been intimidating. But there was a steadiness to the man that helped reassure her.

"What was it that you wanted?" Her voice shook and she had to clear it twice before she felt she finally had control. "Is it about Olya?"

"No." His gaze slipped to the floor for a moment as though he were trying to find the right words to say. "This connection between our two peoples is still new for all of us. From what I've gathered, every Fallen who's formed a connection with their mate has made…mistakes." He chuckled. "Ina would laugh at my choice of words."

"She's your mate?" It shouldn't surprise her that he also was with a human. There was certainly a difference about him from Gadiel and the others, even Eion.

"She is. We both made mistakes while trying to solve a crisis." The hard edge that she'd come to associate with the doctor eased as a smile spread across his face. "You wouldn't have been told, but the reason I created the inhibitor was due to the near system collapse we went through with the stasis tubes from the Kraken. I had no way of waking all the women to save them, without creating chaos with the Fallen mates. You all nearly died."

Kaia shook her head, the realization at how close they'd come to disaster without even realizing hit her hard. "Shit."

"Ina and I had to deal with our relationship, the problems we had adjusting to being thrust together without warning, while trying to save her people. The middle of a crisis isn't the best time to forge a relationship, and yet we somehow managed to do so."

She glanced over at where Eion was talking to Gadiel, painfully aware of the chaos that underpinned both their actions. "Crisis seems to be a fairly normal state of being on this planet."

"True." Hallam gave her hand a quick squeeze before stepping back. "Just know that you will both figure this out. Give it time."

"I'll try." What else could she say? "Thank you."

Hallam nodded before leaving the room. Kaia continued to stand in place, not knowing what to do or how to feel. Yes, this was new to all of them, but Eion had also told her that he didn't want her to come along, even after she'd made it clear she wouldn't stay behind. If that was how their relationship was going to be, then maybe she should try and find a way to sever this bond now before her heart got involved. That would be better for them both.

Gadiel and Eion quickly gathered the few things they had in the room before approaching her. Gadiel handed her what appeared to be a jacket. "We're going to meet Wex and Qwin at the shuttle location. The planet's surface is cold and windy, so you'll need some additional protection."

Eion didn't meet her gaze when she glanced at him. Fine, if that's how things were going to be then she'd play along. "Thank you. Let's go get them."

Without another word, Kaia left the room and walked out of the hole in the side of the medical facility into the unknown.

CHAPTER NINE

The last thing Eion wanted was for Kaia to be on the shuttle with them flying into unspeakable danger. And there *would* be danger – some expected but most resulting from the actions of others while they did what they needed to save the humans.

To save their mates.

Having her by his side meant that Eion's attention would inevitably be divided between doing what was ordered of him and ensuring that nothing harmed her. She might be capable of looking after herself and her sister back on Earth, but she'd barely been out of stasis for a few hours, had been injured, and was still adjusting to him now being a part of her life. Whether she liked that fact or not.

Weixler and Qwin were already at the rendezvous when he, Kaia and Gadiel arrived. Eion couldn't help but be aware of the glances the others cast toward Kaia, no doubt sharing the same concerns that he had, though less certain about their role in her protection.

Gadiel took one of the supply bags from Weixler, not bothering to check its contents before slinging it over his shoulder.

"Zee's giving us a shuttle, but we'll need to make it look like he's not involved. Guard shift change will be soon, we'll make our move then. Move quickly and no injuries."

They all nodded, even Kaia who'd moved to the back of the group. "Is there anything you want me to do?" Her voice was steady, but there was no mistaking her hesitant tone.

"I want you to stay behind with Eion until we give the signal to move. Then run, get onto the shuttle as quickly as possible."

"Keep out of the way." Weixler let out a soft snort. "The last thing we need is you getting yourself killed."

Rage surged through Eion and in a blink he'd thrown himself on Weixler, sending them both crashing to the ground. He didn't remember hitting Weixler, couldn't feel his pain or disorientation through their currently severed cybernetic link. All he saw was the other Fallen's face, the blood that now covered it, the confusion shining from his glowing purple eyes. Eion's throat hurt and it was only then that he realized he was screaming as firm arms pulled him off Weixler's prone body.

He couldn't calm down. The thought of Kaia being hurt, killed, not safe from anyone blinding him with emotions he'd never experienced before. The screams kept coming from him and it wasn't until Kaia knelt in front of him, taking his face in her hands that he started to pull back from the abyss of madness.

"Eion, I'm here. There's nothing wrong. No one hurt me. I'm safe." She spoke softly, but he had no difficulty hearing her, even if her words took longer for his mind to process.

He became vaguely aware of the others helping Weixler to his feet, could feel the weight of their gazes on him. Eion tried to calm the rage, tried to get control of himself, closing his eyes to focus his attention on Kaia's touch and her soft litany of words.

"Eion, I'm okay. No one is going to hurt me because you're here to make sure that doesn't happen. And the others are going to make sure I'm safe too. They're your squad, your team, and they wouldn't want you to suffer or see anything bad happen to me. They'll protect me the same way you're going to protect their mates when we find them. Isn't that right?"

"Yes." The single word came out as little more than a croak, but he finally felt as though he were regaining a small measure of his control.

She increased the hold on his face and leaned in close enough that he could have easily kissed her. "That's right. You're going to take some nice deep breaths. I don't want you to think about anything else until we get this under control."

It didn't take him long to ease the tension in his body as the unexpected burst of anger receded. "Wex?"

Weixler stood just behind Kaia. "I forgot that you're not under the influence of Hallam's injections. I will mind my words going forward."

"No, I shouldn't have – "

Weixler held up his hand. "I suspect you'll need to offer me the same courtesy when we locate my mate. We're all adjusting."

Qwin slung one of the other supply bags over his shoulder. "We need to move now. The shift change is coming, and we need to get there and into position before our window of opportunity passes. We'll only have a few moments to do this if we want to ensure no one gets hurt."

Kaia moved and held out her hands for Eion to take. "I'll stay behind you the whole time."

Her fingers were smaller than his, her hands far more delicate than most of the Grus women he'd known in his life. The touch of her skin against his snapped his attention back to how small her body was, but her inner strength was something that he needed to not discount. Kaia was his to protect, but he was also hers to watch over.

Getting to his feet, they fell into position and made their move toward the shuttle. His mind was hyper focused on everything around them: their positions relative to the shuttle, Kaia's stride length and how she slowly fell behind them as they moved across the rocky terrain. Once they reached their destination, he became aware of the position of the last guard closest to the shuttle, and how he'd be the one who'd spot their group if he were to turn his head even slightly in their direction.

Gadiel lifted his blaster, having it trained on the spot behind the guards. "Proxima alpha."

Eion's matrix pulled the battle plan up and he moved without thinking. Gadiel fired three shots behind the guards, sending them running for cover as Weixler used a code breaker tool to force the shuttle doors open. Eion grabbed Kaia as the guards returned fire, using his body as a shield when the shots landed uncomfortably close to where she stood.

As quickly as their assault began, the doors to the shuttle opened and they were safely inside. They didn't need their cybernetic link to know exactly what each of them had to do next; their vast experience ensuring those tasks were fully ingrained years ago. Eion moved Kaia to a seat toward the back of the shuttle but still well within his line of sight. "Stay here. Buckle in."

She nodded, looking far less confident than she had back at the medical building. "I won't move a muscle."

Eion didn't have time to say anything else and moved to assist Gadiel. He fell into the co-pilot's seat, checking the readings on the scanners. "So far there's been no response from the prison's security system."

"Zee won't be able to delay that much longer." Gadiel engaged the thrusters, lifting the shuttle off the ground with a shake. "Hold on."

Eion raised the shields as Weixler brought the weapons online. They wouldn't fire on anyone unless it was necessary, and even if they did, Eion knew it wouldn't be to do any serious harm. Eion's eyes never left the scanner, anticipating fire any moment – but thankfully nothing came. "Zee must have been able to delay any system retaliation."

"He'll pay a price for that." Gadiel tensed. "Now we need to break free of the planet's atmosphere."

The shuttle hit turbulence as it reached the cloud layer, the ever-present electrical storm that raged in the atmosphere from the environmental damage that the Sholle had done to Zarlan. The storms normally acted as a type of defence shield against any unwanted visitors to the surface, their intensity enough to destroy lesser shielded ships. The Fallen had long ago established a flight pattern between Zarlan and Grus Prime that allowed for the least amount of turbulence en route to the space station.

They were not going that path.

"Hold on, everyone!" Gadiel maneuvered the shuttle through a storm, lightening bolts cascading in the sky around them. "Eion, keep an eye on those shields. We won't be able to take many direct hits."

Despite knowing they could die at a moment's notice – or perhaps because of that – Eion couldn't help but be worried about Kaia. He wanted to be with her, to wrap his arms around her and promise that they'd get through this, that everything and everyone would be okay. The blips on the scanner, indications of their aft shield weakening, the shudders brought about by the electrical storm around them, *everything* seemed secondary to the waves of fear and nervousness emanating from Kaia.

He needed to go to her. Needed to reassure her.

Gadiel's hand shot out and grabbed hold of his arm. Eion looked up and was shocked to see his leader and friend shaking his head. "I need you here for a few more moments. We're almost through."

Right, yes. He could do this, needed to do this so he could ensure Kaia's safety. Just a bit longer and everything would be okay. She'd be okay. With his attention back where it needed to be, Eion was able to modulate the shields in time to block another lightning blast to the shuttle's aft section. After another few tense moments, they shifted above the cloud cover and out into the upper stratosphere.

Silence washed over them as the darkness of space stretched before them. Gadiel let out a soft sigh as he leaned back in his seat. "Weixler, see if you can locate the Black Guard shuttle that took our mates."

"Already searching."

Eion performed a system check, cringing at the damage. "This shuttle is passable at best. We have limited weapons and shields. It will get us where we need to go, but if we take any heavy fire, I'm not certain how well we'll hold up."

"Then I'll make sure we don't get hit." Gadiel nodded toward the back. "I've got this. Go check on her."

Eion didn't need to be told twice. With his attention no longer divided, he was overcome by Kaia's emotional turmoil. Qwin was sitting beside her, holding a cloth to her head. He didn't move, not even when Eion let out a soft growl and stood over them both. "What happened?"

"A weapon from one of the supply bags wasn't secure. It went flying in the turbulence and hit the side of her head. I'm making sure there isn't any additional damage." Qwin looked up at him as he spoke the last part, his gaze steeled. "I'll stop touching her if you want."

"I'm right fucking here you know." Kaia jerked away from Qwin, taking the cloth from his hands to reapply the pressure. "He needs to learn that not everyone who comes close to me needs to have their ass kicked."

"Are you okay?" The tension that had built inside Eion eased at Kaia's annoyance. If she was that angry at him, then any harm that had come to her was unlikely to be serious.

"I'm fine." Her gaze darted to his for a moment before she returned her attention to Qwin. "Do you think I need more of those nanobots?"

"You shouldn't. They're already working to stem the bleeding, so I suspect you'll be better before we reach deep space."

"Thanks." Kaia watched as Qwin got up and moved to the front of the shuttle. She didn't look back at Eion, not even when he sat beside her. "So now what do we do?"

He wanted her to look him in the eyes so he could see her concern, rather than simply feel it wash over him. He had to fight to hold himself back from taking her chin in his hand to do that. "Weixler will locate the path the Black Guard's shuttle took and we'll follow them. Then we'll get your sister back."

Kaia's chin lowered as her lips turned down into a frown. "Promise?"

"I promise you." This time he didn't hold back and pulled her into his arms. Having her there, feeling the warmth of her body against his somehow made everything feel better. "I already told you. The Qadrus is an elite squad sent to do missions that no one else would dare attempt. We've been deep in enemy territory on rescue missions before. Recovered stolen technology. There was even a time we stole a military frigate from the Caldarins. Getting your sister and the others back safely will be the easiest thing we've ever done."

Kaia chuckled, leaning into his side. "That's reassuring. I never thought in a million years I'd need a crack strike force to help me out halfway across the galaxy, only a short time after having come out of stasis. If someone had told me that back on Earth, I wouldn't have believed them."

"If someone had told me a week ago that I'd be leaving the planet with my alien mate to go rescue her sister from the Black Guard, I would have laughed in their face."

Kaia sat up and looked at him wide-eyed. "Wait, I'm the alien? Oh my god, I hadn't even thought of that." She burst out laughing.

The others all looked at her, confused expressions, and curious glances. Eion would have reacted the same if it weren't for the fact that he felt her relief and joy. He hadn't realized that he too was laughing until Kaia smiled his way. "You're very handsome when you laugh."

Handsome? That wasn't something he ever remembered another person said to him.

Cupping her face, he soaked in the warmth of her skin against his touch. "You're the only one to ever think so."

Maybe if everything went the way he hoped and they survived this, they'd have an actual chance at a proper relationship.

Maybe things were finally starting to change for him.

CHAPTER TEN

At some point during the hours they'd been traveling toward Olya and the others, Kaia had fallen asleep. She only knew this because one moment she was sitting with her head against Eion's shoulder, and then in the next she was lying down on what appeared to be a small cot. The surface was hard and not particularly comfortable, but it felt good to be in a position where she could relax and catch her breath, even if it was only for a moment.

It was nearly impossible to process everything that had happened to her since waking up from stasis. Even before then if she were being honest. Their last few days on Earth before they'd boarded the Kraken had been chaotic at best; she'd tried to comfort and reassure her parents that they'd find the solution to Olya's condition in space, while ignoring her own niggling feeling that there was something else going on, something selfish that was pulling her to make this journey. Olya, who didn't always agree with Kaia's plans, strangely hadn't protested at all when told about the Kraken's journey. At least Kaia now knew why, making her guilt easier to deal with.

There couldn't have been any way Kaia had known about

Eion and the others, no way to anticipate his presence and their apparent connection. If Kaia had known, she would have thought twice about leaving Earth, or at the very least would have found a way to ensure her sister was cared for first.

Kaia always felt she had to put her own needs second.

No one had ever forced her to do so – not her parents and certainly not Olya – but Kaia always knew in her heart that was the right thing to do. As the healthy twin, she'd never felt there was any other option. Not until the door opened back at the medical facility and she saw Eion for the first time. In that moment Kaia had wanted nothing other than him, wanted to be selfish, to leave Olya to the doctors who no doubt were more than capable of easing her condition so Kaia could run off with a man she'd only just laid eyes on.

What kind of horrible person did that make her?

The low rumble of voices finally penetrated the sleep fog her brain was still under, pulling her out of her self-deprecating funk and back into the present. They were on their way to God only knew where, to rescue Olya and the others from the space mob. And what a fucked-up thought that was. There was no way she could have anticipated there being a space mob, let alone the idea that they'd kidnap her sister for unknown reasons.

Why did they break into the medical facility and take them?

Sitting up, Kaia sucked in a breath and stretched against the aches that still lingered in her body. Hopefully those nanobots would be able to help her with that because she wasn't certain they had any other painkillers available to them out here. The cot was behind a small hallway that offered a modicum of privacy in the otherwise open shuttle. It wasn't big enough for more than one person, and certainly didn't look wide enough to accommodate Eion and his bulky cybernetics. Getting to her feet, she became immediately aware of him and his annoyance. She felt the dueling desires of him needing to concentrate and wanting to throw her back down on that cot and have sex with her.

The blush that heated her face came out of nowhere and made her instantly self conscious. Eion stood up from the co-pilot's chair and faced her. She knew he was able to sense her emotions, probably far stronger than she could his, and no doubt wanted to make sure that she was okay. Her gaze was locked on his glowing green eyes when Weixler stood up quickly, bumping into him. "*Fraking* move."

"I'm obviously here." Eion's eyebrow lifted so high, she was surprised it hadn't left his face. "Watch where you're going."

"I was. You're here focused on her instead of your job!"

Eion turned to Weixler, his anger palpable to Kaia. "You insubordinate *sharalla*."

The tension in the small cockpit jumped to max within a heartbeat, and Kaia could only watch as they faced off. Weixler used his cybernetic hand to grab Eion by the shirt and throw him out of the way. Eion moved but remained on his feet and immediately grabbed Weixler by the throat. She knew there was nothing she could do to stop them from fighting, and yet she was racing across the small shuttle to try her best to pull Eion off Weixler. "Stop!"

"Enough!" Gadiel roared, got to his feet, and grabbed them both. "We don't have time for the two of you to lose control."

"He's sitting here with his mate, unfocused on his tasks and unwilling to do what needs to be done to save the others." Weixler's words came out in short, sharp bites that dug into Kaia's very soul. "It's probably for the best that we're not connected through the link right now. I couldn't stomach hearing you moon over your mate."

"That's not fair." Kaia stepped away from the group, her sudden anger directed toward them all. "You have no right to blame Eion or myself for anything. We didn't ask for this mating any more than you did with yours. None of the women were even thinking about wanting to find a mate, let alone get caught up in whatever the hell is going on between your people and the fucking space mob."

Eion dropped his hold on Weixler and moved toward her. "Don't be upset."

"Pardon me?" Rage raced through her. "I'm worried sick about my sister and you're getting involved in a fight because you're all horny. If this is what its going to be like being mated to your people, then maybe once I find Olya we'll get a shuttle of our own and fly off where we can start over!"

The four cyborgs all fell silent, staring at her. Her temper might not be something that reared up often, but when it did anyone within twenty meters knew enough to back off and head for cover. To their credit the men all looked wary of her response to their actions, which only served to embolden her.

"You all seem to forget that we didn't ask for this, didn't come here looking for you. Yes, I know there was something that spoke to me that reassured me that my decision to bring my sister out here to look for a cure was the right decision, but you can't know that it was because of you. And even if it was, that doesn't mean you get to treat us like possessions for you to use and fight over. We're living beings with hopes, fears, and dreams of our own. So, smarten up or fuck off!"

Eion was grinning at the end of her tirade. "You heard my mate. It seems we need to alter our behavior or else suffer the wrath of our mates."

"Human women are a formidable bunch." Qwin chuckled. "I hope my mate is able to put me in my place the way you have, Kaia."

Dammit, they weren't supposed to agree with her. Letting out a growl, she turned and retreated to the cot. The last thing she wanted was to deal with a group of arrogant men. She'd had more than enough of that living back on Earth. She was aware of Eion trailing after her, his amusement bouncing inside her head as though it was being directly beamed there.

It only served to piss her off more. She waited until he was close enough to nearly touch her when she spun around and pointed her finger at him, stopping him dead in his tracks. "You don't get to laugh at me. You don't get to make light of what I'm feeling. You don't get to downplay my emotional response to a situation that's outside of my control."

The amusement that rolled off Eion stopped as quickly as it had reared up. "My apologies."

His contrition took some of the heat out of her emotional turmoil. "Accepted. But you need to understand that humans don't take kindly to being belittled. We might not all speak out about it, some of us let it quietly fester. Your amusement at my genuine anger and fears about the state of my sister is wrong. I won't accept that from anyone, let alone someone who claims to be my soul mate."

Kaia's anger had mostly petered out by the time she'd finished speaking. The look of contrition on Eion's face matched what she felt coming from him through whatever this bond was between them. Embarrassment at her outburst threatened to claim her, but for once in her life she pushed that response away. She was perfectly within her rights to stand up for herself and demand that these aliens respond to her the way she deserved. It wasn't the sort of thing she would have said to anyone back on Earth, even if she should have on more than one occasion.

She'd spent so much of her life looking after Olya, ensuring that her physical and emotional needs were looked after, Kaia tended to ignore her own wants and desires. She knew she had a martyr complex that if left unchecked would fester beneath the surface, making her miserable when no one acknowledged what she did for them. She hated that part of herself, hated that she wished she'd been the one born with a life-threatening illness so someone would look after her for once.

What kind of person did that make her?

She was caught off guard when Eion pulled her into his arms.

The press of his cybernetic arm against her body no longer felt as foreign as it first had, instead offering a grounding point to help anchor her spiraling thoughts. Wrapping her arms around his chest, she let go of the tension that had built inside her. "I'm so scared."

"I know. I'm sorry I hadn't realized that sooner." He tightened his grip on her. "I'm aware of your emotional state, feel the waves of conflicting emotions coming off you. I haven't had to deal with emotions since before my death and rebirth. Even before then, I wasn't particularly good at...feelings."

Kaia pulled back enough so she could look him in the eyes. "Aerin had mentioned that. That all the Fallen had died and were brought back to life. I can't even imagine what that must have been like for you to deal with."

"Both dying and the rebirth were outside of my control." He shrugged. "But not many creatures have a second chance at life. I tried to do everything I could to help my people, to make the best use that I could of this second chance."

Would she have reacted the same if she'd been put in that position? Kaia couldn't be sure.

Eion brushed a strand of her hair from her face. "We'll get your sister back. She and the other women will have a chance to be with their mates and maybe for once in our lives we'll be able to have something more than death and fear."

"That would be a miracle." The thought of not only Olya being finally healthy, but for her to have the chance of living her own life, it equally excited and terrified her.

"What's wrong?" He pulled away to look her in the eyes.

"Nothing." She knew he was able to feel her trepidation and she couldn't bring herself to lie to him. "It's just, if Olya has a mate of her own, if we're finally able to cure her of the Breneman's virus...she...won't need me anymore."

"Is that the totality of your relationship? You caring for her?"

"No." The moments when Olya was feeling okay and they'd

spend the nights talking and laughing were few and far between. Kaia cherished every one of them. "But why would she want to spend time with me when she can go out and finally live a life of her own?"

Eion cupped her face with his cybernetic hand, and once again she was surprised by its feel against her skin. "You're allowed to have a life beyond her."

Am I?

His fingers flexed on her cheek. "I've rarely wanted anything or anyone for myself. I'd sworn my life in service of my people long before I'd become Fallen. But I knew when I first saw you that if given a chance, I'd choose you instead."

Her breath caught in her lungs. *I'd choose you instead.*

"Eion, I…" *Yes.*

The sound of Gadiel clearing his throat drew her attention. "I'm sorry for interrupting, but we know where they're taking the women." He sounded less than pleased.

"What's wrong?" She pulled away from Eion, though she reached for his hand, not wanting to break contact completely.

The line of Gadiel's mouth tightened briefly. "They're heading to Druuxa."

"*Frak.*" Eion squeezed her hand briefly before moving back toward the cockpit. "How long do you estimate they'll be on the surface before we can intercept?"

"Wait, what's on Druuxa?" The tension in the shuttle was palpable. "Are they going to be okay?"

Qwin moved to her side and guided her to the seat closest to the cockpit. "It's where the Black Guard are headquartered. The entire planet is basically a fortress that no one gets in or out of without them knowing."

Great. "So how the hell are we going to rescue them?"

"We'll come up with a plan and get them back." Qwin gave her knee a squeeze as he stood, his black hair slipping forward to mute the blue glow of his eyes. "They made a mistake when they took our mates."

"Why's that?"

Eion turned to face her, his grin chilling. "Parents use threats of the Black Guard taking them in the dark of night to scare their children. But our squad? Tales of what we can do scare the Black Guard."

Kaia didn't know why, but that was both the most unnerving and reassuring thing she'd ever heard in her life. "What do we do next?"

Eion turned and took her by the shoulders, as his gaze narrowed. "We follow them there."

THERE WASN'T much Kaia was able to do in the ensuing hour it took for them to approach the planet. The cyborgs strategized and prepared, while all she was able to do was sit by and watch. She couldn't imagine how much help she was going to be once they finally landed, but she wasn't going to sit by and do nothing.

Was she?

The sensors on Weixler's screen sounded. "Hold on, we're heading in."

She slipped into the seat restraints and held in her surprised yelp at the sudden turbulence. If she wanted to be there for Olya, then she was going to have to prove to the others that she could look after herself. They didn't need any additional distractions and she wasn't going to do anything that would interfere with the rescue operation.

"We have to assume that they're expecting us." Gadiel's attention was locked on the screen in front of him. "Even if we manage to slip beneath their sensors and land, we'll have limited time for reconnaissance and rescue."

"We'll also need to ensure the shuttle is secured for our

escape." Weixler glanced at Kaia. "We also can't know their current physical and mental states. The longer we're stuck on Druuxa the worse it is for everyone."

Despite him not looking at her, Kaia could feel Eion's concern for her as clearly as if it were her own. She tightened her grip on the restraints. "Do you think the Black Guard will harm them?"

"No." Gadiel glanced back at her. "They're too valuable as negotiation chits."

"The longer they have them, the faster that value drops." Qwin shook his head. "We need to get in and out quickly."

She wanted nothing more than to hit the ground running and save her sister. She'd been the one to look after her, even more so than their parents, since Kaia first learned there was something different about her twin. Having to put her trust in strangers to do what she couldn't was the single hardest thing she'd encountered in her life. When Eion looked back at her once again, Kaia knew in her heart that this was the right thing. "I trust you all to get them back safe."

Eion's smile lightened her heart. "Then let's do this."

CHAPTER ELEVEN

Eion wanted nothing more than to put Kaia in a room, lock the door and ensure that no one would be able to get inside to hurt her. It was the worst kind of impulse and not helpful given they were currently flying directly into the heart of Black Guard territory. There'd be no way to hide her, and he realized now that doing so would sell Kaia and her abilities short. She might not be as physically strong as a Fallen, nor familiar with this region of space and the dangers that existed here, but she was smart and insightful and knew the other women better than any of them. She'd be able to anticipate their likely reactions to the situation, and her presence would be reassuring to the women once they located and rescued them.

All he had to do was make sure she didn't get herself killed.

Gadiel's maneuvers with the shuttle pushed the stabilizers to their limits. They shadowed the moves of a large transport heading to the surface, staying inside the sensor dark spot generated by the transport's energy shields. Eion forced his attention away from monitoring Kaia's emotional state so he could hack into the transport's communication array.

"I'm in. We can monitor incoming transmissions and I can

force my way into the Guard's systems. We'll know if they spot us."

"If they're using similar protocols as they have in the past, they'll move the women separately to their final location and do as little to draw attention to themselves as possible." Weixler leaned forward and Eion knew he was already perfecting a tactical plan. "It appears they've landed at Trytan space port. That makes our job easier."

"Why's that?" Kaia's voice was still an anomaly in their long familiar group.

"Lots of people coming and going." Weixler's tone was flat, another indication he was deep in his planning. "It will be easier for us to blend into the crowd and do what we need to do."

Eion could feel that Kaia wanted to ask more questions, but she remained silent.

They focused on their maneuvers and the crucial next few moments. The odds of the security net detecting them was nearly half, and if that happened then they'd have no choice but to go in blasters firing; retreat wasn't an option. Eion's gaze was locked on the sensors, his matrix analysing every communication thread bouncing from the planet to all the ships on entry or departure.

Nothing.

"We may have gotten lucky and flown under their sensors." He barely spoke but knew the others had heard him regardless. "Gad, you'll need to adjust your approach vector by two degrees."

"Done."

"Qwin, shift the supplies to the travel packs. We'll have to hit the ground running."

"Done."

"Wex, send the plan to the ship's computer."

"Done."

"Everyone download it to your matrix. We'll have to assume coms blackout between us for the duration of the mission."

"What do you want me to do?"

The sound of Kaia's voice jerked Eion out of his mission trance. He didn't want her doing anything but that wasn't realistic either. There was nothing worse than being the one left behind and having nothing to occupy one's mind. "When we land, I'll show you some key functions on the shuttle. We'll need you to run emergency communications for us and be able to get this shuttle in the air in case we need to leave in a hurry. Think you can handle that?"

The grin on her face told him all he needed to know. "I'm a fast learner."

Silence fell on them as Gadiel matched the transport ship moves until the last possible moment. Eion held his breath, despite his matrix analyzing their vector and knowing they'd make it. There was always the chance that something unexpected could happen, something that would knock everything off course.

Like unexpectedly being told that you now had a mate.

Eion waited until they passed the final sensor check before he finalized his hack of the Trytan mainframe. "I've secured a landing location for us. It's the closest I could manage to where they brought our mates without drawing attention to our arrival."

"I see it." Gadiel changed their direction and within moments, set the shuttle down on the small landing pad.

They weren't the only ones here, the pad large enough to accommodate three shuttles in total. That meant there were more eyes they'd have to avoid when they left the ship, but it would help them blend in with the surrounding environment. Without having to ask for it, Weixler sent a ship summary of the other vessels. "One is a Black Guard carrier. Empty and not scheduled to depart for two days. The other is a Maytar supply skid. They'll be leaving once they've unloaded their goods."

"They'll keep their distance." Gadiel got to his feet and took one of the supply bags from Qwin. "Eion, you have five minutes to show her what needs to be done. Then we have to leave." He pointed at Weixler and Qwin and they quickly left the shuttle.

Kaia was already in the pilot's chair before he had a chance to say anything. "What do I do?"

There was a quiver in her voice and her face had gone pale, matching the sudden burst of nerves that came off her in waves. He hated this. Hated knowing that he couldn't stay with her but couldn't realistically bring her along either. She might be capable and perceptive, but she wasn't a soldier. He had to leave her behind for everyone's safety.

"Computer, grant full access to Kaia. Communications and pilot controls."

There was a soft beep. "Granted."

Eion took a breath, stood and moved so he was directly behind her chair. "It's simple. This button here is communications. This one will start the shuttle. And this one over here will fire the weapons. You can verbally interface with the computer to get the settings you need. Maintain communication silence until you hear from us. If there's an emergency, hit that button and tell me."

"Comms, flight, weapons." She brushed her fingertip over each one, nodding as she did. "Got it. Keep silent unless there's a problem and try not to worry."

There was something else in her voice beyond the nerves he couldn't quite place. "What?"

"I should be going with you." She turned awkwardly in the seat to look up at him. "I'm useless here."

"You're safe here."

"I know how to fire a blaster and I'm more than capable of keeping up with you. I need to be there to save Olya."

"Kaia, you know that's not – "

"Why not!" She shoved him back, angry, and scared. The tears on her cheek broke his heart. "She needs me."

"I promise, we'll get her back safely."

"Eion." Gadiel's voice reached him from outside the shuttle. "We need to leave."

"I'm coming." Eion shoved his emotions deep down. He couldn't risk the mission by having his attention focused on Kaia. "Comms, flight, weapons."

Ignoring the rush of fear and anger that came off her, he turned his back and left the shuttle.

"Everything all right?" Weixler lifted an eyebrow. "She going to do what we need her to?"

Eion grabbed the remaining supply pack from Qwin and strode away. "Let's go."

Kaia's heart pounded so hard she was terrified that she'd pass out from the stress. Sweat covered her palms, forcing her to constantly wipe them on her thighs to dry them. The last thing she wanted was to need to move quickly and have her fingers slip and hit the wrong button. That would be her fucking luck.

Eion and the others had only been gone for a few minutes, but she was already worried that something horrible had happened to them. Aliens walked around the platform, moving back and forth from the supply shuttle with loads of goods for the city. If she'd harbored any doubt that she'd left Earth and was now on an alien world, the sight of these creatures would have quickly dispelled the notion. Large red bug-like men, handily carrying crates that appeared large enough to fit all four of the cyborgs, lumbered between the shuttle and skid, nearly out of her view from the pilot's seat. They were being directed by a super tall woman, with iridescent skin and flowing purple hair that went down to her feet. Others moved around, but Kaia didn't dare move much for fear of drawing unwanted attention to herself.

She needed to keep a low profile because she got the feeling that if someone found out she was here, there wouldn't be time for Eion to come to the rescue.

God, she hoped they weren't long finding Olya and the others. Prayed that the women were being held safe until they could break them out, or bust in, whatever they needed to do to get her sister back to her in one piece. And then she'd have a long talk with Eion about leaving her behind like this.

Kaia didn't care if he needed to teach her how to use weapons, sneak around, or use self-defence, she wanted to know. Hell, she'd even consider getting cybernetic implants if it meant she'd be able to keep her loved ones safe. Her gaze landed on the tall woman and Kaia realized that Olya wouldn't need her the same way once they got her back. Qwin had seemed adamant that the nanobots would be able to cure her of Breneman's virus, and then she'd have her mate who would apparently be unable to keep his hands off her. If everything that Aerin had told them was true, then Olya would finally have someone other than herself who'd love her unconditionally. No doubt she'd love that, which meant Kaia would have more time on her hands than she'd know what to do with.

Eion will know how to fill it.

She shivered as memories of their hard and fast lovemaking back at the medical facility flashed through her head. In the quiet and alien environment, those thoughts comforted her as much as they threatened to arouse. For that brief moment, while she'd wanted nothing more than to prove to him that she was able to take care of herself, he'd touched her as though she were the most precious thing in the universe. It was so easy then to dismiss everything but wanting to get Olya back, but sitting here alone with nothing but her thoughts as company made it hard to ignore the connection she felt growing between them.

If Olya doesn't need you anymore, maybe you can finally focus on someone for yourself.

Her mother would have laughed at the thought of Kaia *actu-*

ally putting her needs before someone else's. She'd always teased Kaia that she didn't need to worry about being Olya's mother because Kaia did everything for her instead. Kaia had always taken that as a compliment, even when Olya told her that their mom felt hurt sometimes when she wasn't the one there for her. She couldn't change that now and all she could hope was that their parents had been happy after they'd left Earth, and that they'd lived their best lives.

A large bang on the landing platform caught her attention, and Kaia leaned forward to try and catch a glance at what was going on. One of the large alien bug men had dropped a container and was currently being yelled at by the woman. *I guess bosses yelling at employees is a universal condition.* Did the mob even have employees? There was still so much she didn't know about her new world, and Kaia hated feeling naive. Once they found the others, she really did want to take time to discover all she could about their new home.

Settling back into her seat, Kaia tried to relax and give the nanobots time to heal the remaining aches and pains that still lingered. So much had happened in such a short period of time, her body was exhausted. She must have drifted off briefly because the next time she heard a loud bang she sat straight up, her feet slamming to the floor. It took her a moment to realize that the sound hadn't come from the landing pad like the last one had. The banging echoed once more as she turned to look at the shuttle's locked door.

Someone was trying to get inside.

CHAPTER TWELVE

They moved silently through the crowded streets, their faces down to avoid eye contact with passers-by. This was standard operating procedure, and it was second nature to Eion. What wasn't normal was the swirl of emotions – both his and Kaia's – that were bouncing around inside his head, a constant press and chatter of thoughts and feelings that grew in prominence with each passing hour.

How had any of the other cyborg mates functioned with this level of distraction going on in their minds? Rykal had negotiated a unification agreement with the Grus, and he too was mated to a human. If the rumors were to be believed, they had a connection so strong he'd felt her presence on a spaceship the moment it had entered their sector of space. And somehow, he'd moved past this insanity and still functioned like a normal member of Fallen society.

Maybe Eion wasn't as resilient as he liked to give himself credit.

Or maybe Rykal had accepted his mate for who she was and what she brought him, rather than try to push her away.

His body kept moving alongside Gadiel and the others, even

as he had to mentally force himself to keep pace. He wasn't holding Kaia away. He'd stated that he wanted nothing more than for her to be with him, to share his bed. Yes, she was a distraction, and he ran the risk of not being able to perform his duties the way that he should, but they'd find a way to make that work. He'd ensure she was safe and secure when he'd be out on assignment, and he'd find a way to keep all thoughts of her locked away.

Gadiel led them down a small alleyway and motioned for Weixler and Qwin to continue. As Eion moved to slip past as well, Gadiel pressed his hand to Eion's chest, stopping him dead. "I don't know what's going on with you, but you need to focus."

Eion narrowed his gaze, not liking the annoyance he saw reflected in Gadiel's red gaze. "I'm focused."

"On what? Based on your uneven steps and breathing, it's not on this mission."

He hadn't realized he'd had such a strong physiological response to being separated from her. "Kaia is a part of this mission as much as the others are."

"She's safe on the shuttle. I need you here so we can get the others free." Gadiel slid his hand to Eion's shoulder. "She needs you to get her sister safe."

"And what happens if we can't do that?" It had been the one lingering question he'd had scraping the back of his mind since they'd started out on this mission. How would his mate react if they weren't able to save her sister?

Would she ever forgive him for that failure? Eion wasn't certain he would.

Gadiel squeezed his shoulder hard. "We won't fail. Not those women and not ourselves. We're a team and no one has ever bested us. Not even death stopped us from doing what needed to be done. The Black Guard certainly won't be the first."

It was that sense of purpose that had always driven Eion forward, even before his rebirth. He'd taken pleasure in being useful to others, doing the extreme things they were incapable of doing. Kaia needed her sister back, so Eion would save her.

Nodding once, he felt his mind shift yet again. Knowing he was able to feel her emotions, he could only assume that she was at least partially aware of his state of being as well. If he were projecting doubts and fears, he could only imagine she was feeling that too. Closing his eyes, Eion took a deep breath and pushed out a blast of renewed confidence he hoped Kaia felt. Opening them once more, he nodded. "Let's get them back."

Weixler and Qwin were waiting for them at the end of the alley, Qwin giving Eion a small reassuring smile. "Based on the sensor readings, I think our women are in the building on the other side of this square."

The street before them was busy, but it was easy to pick out the Black Guard sentries patrolling outside of a fortified front door of one of the buildings. Eion tried to use his enhanced vision to get a reading on how many people were inside, but there was some sort of shielding going on that made the scan impossible. "Any idea of what's going on in there?"

"I've sent a drone in." Weixler had been busy using a control pad. "I hate not having access to the cybernetic link. These controls are *fraking* clumsy."

"Do the best you can." Gadiel ducked his head around the corner. "I see at least fifteen Black Guard sentries in the square. I assume they haven't detected our presence if they have so few out on patrol."

"That won't last long." Eion knew as soon as they located the women, their group would need to split up for multiple entry points. "If we're lucky, they won't realize we've got them until we're halfway back to the shuttle."

"The drone is in." Weixler turned the control panel around for the rest of them to see. "They're holding the women on the second floor in a room with minimal security. It's either the most obvious trap in the universe, or they're only going to be here briefly until they can get them somewhere more secure."

Gadiel looked the readings over before handing them to Eion. "We'll have to assume both things. They must know that the Fallen would come after these women and are planning to apprehend us. We have to also assume that they're not fools and wouldn't plan to keep the women there without adequate protection long term."

Eion quickly reviewed the building layout and identified all the possible ambush areas. "Gad, if you and Wex go in through the ventilation on the roof, Qwin and I can come in through the storage room at the south end of the building. We should be able to breach simultaneously, get the women and get out before they realize we're in the building."

They shared a look and Eion knew they were all thinking the same thing. If the Black Guard realized what was happening, there was a very real chance that they wouldn't get out of there alive.

Gadiel narrowed his gaze and lowered his voice. "No matter what happens, we'll get them out. We'll get them back to Zarlan and start our new lives with our mates."

It was strange having Gadiel acknowledge the precious status of the women – their mates. Eion hadn't considered that they'd no longer be a team, be sent off for missions that benefited the lives of the Grus and the Fallen. Would it be enough for him, putting all his energy into ensuring Kaia had the best possible life in this new place she'd traveled so far to reach?

Of course, it will be.

In that moment, it was as though everything slotted into place in Eion's mind. The shift was subtle, but he knew that it was the right and perfect thing. He would have a new life with Kaia, new goals and dreams to reach for. He no longer needed to give everything in his heart and soul to benefit others who'd never been aware of his presence. For once in a long while, he could focus his attention on the things that he wanted for himself.

He wanted Kaia. He wanted to be happy.

"Eion?" Qwin's voice was full of concern that was so unlike anything the medic had ever expressed before. Clearly, Eion wasn't the only one emotionally impacted. "You okay?"

He nodded. "Be thankful the three of you had a second shot of the inhibitor. These emotions take some getting used to."

Weixler snorted. "Maybe I'll ask Hallam for a third one if that's how I'm going to respond."

"Enough." Gadiel shoved the drone's control pad back at Weixler. "Grab your gear. We're moving out. Communication blackout until we reach the breach point."

"Understood." Eion slipped his blaster and two sonic grenades into his pockets, watching Qwin do the same. "Let's move."

He didn't need to wait and see if Qwin was with him, knowing the medic was already on his flank. They moved quickly along the perimeter of the square, keeping out of sight of the nearest patrol, while crossing the street to reach the alley just south of their destination. Eion's matrix held the layout of the building, and it took him a moment to plot out the best approach vector that led to the storage room window.

Unlike the previous alley, this one had several people huddled together, their dirty faces and malnourished bodies seemingly one with the pitted and worn stone exterior of the building they leaned against for support. Another symptom of the Black Guard and how their hold on this sector had grown since the Grus had withdrawn over half a century ago. Eion could only hope things would improve for everyone now that unification had occurred and both the Fallen and the Grus were now positioned to reassert themselves as a force for good in the sector.

He felt Qwin hesitate as they passed, and Eion knew the medic wanted nothing more than to make sure they were okay. If everything went the way he wanted and they got the women out undetected, Eion would ensure they came back this way so Qwin could check them over.

They approached the back of the building with no difficulty, and it only took Eion a few minutes to interrupt the security sensor long enough for them to climb inside. It was unnerving how easily it had been to get into the building, which only reaffirmed the idea that they were walking headfirst into a trap.

"Keep your sensors wide." Eion pulled his blaster out. "I don't like this."

"Far too easy." Qwin followed suit. "I don't know if its due to the closer proximity, or if the inhibitor is starting to wear off, but I'm growing more aware of her emotions. I can almost hear her thoughts." There was a strange note in Qwin's voice, something that Eion recognized as the odd sensation of having that intimate connection with someone who wasn't a cyborg.

"Who's your mate?" Eion's voice was soft, quiet in a way that went against his normally firm personality.

"Olya. I believe it's Olya." He looked at Eion and smiled. "I suspect that means we'll be spending more time together once we're back to safety."

"They do seem abnormally close." Life after this felt more and more like a promise of something pure. "Let's get this over with."

His own connection with Kaia was quiet – *had she fallen asleep? Was she okay?* – which allowed him to better focus on the task at hand. Turning, Eion tried once again to scan the corridor through the wall using his enhanced vision. This time, he was able to faintly detect three heat signatures as they passed and turned a corner, heading in the direction they needed to go. "Whatever they're using to block our scans, has a gap in coverage. I have limited close-proximity range. We're clear, but I can't say for how long."

Stepping out into the corridor, Eion calculated the fastest route to the second floor. There was a service transportation tube designed to move large crates from the roof to the main area. The trio of Black Guard members had moved past it, giving them a brief window of opportunity. Eion moved with Qwin directly behind him. It only took a moment for the transportation tube doors to open, but once they were inside the rest of the controls were locked down.

"If I try to override this it will alert security." Eion looked around and noticed a hatch on the ceiling. "We climb."

"Wonderful." Qwin had never been a fan of heights, though his fears had been tamped down significantly once he'd been reborn. It didn't stop him from yanking the hatch down to pull himself up. "We'll have to use the pipes to climb."

"I'm behind you." Eion's frame was nearly too wide to make it through the hatch, but with some shifting he was able to manage and pulled the hatch shut behind him.

They moved quickly and silently, not knowing exactly how much time they'd have before someone called the transport tube. There was little extra space for them to maneuver and the last thing Eion wanted was to be crushed to death. Kaia would never forgive him.

Qwin reached the second-floor door and began looking for a latch. "There's a ventilation shaft we can enter. I just need to get the cover off."

"Work fast." Eion hated being this *fraking* exposed.

"Give me a minute." It took longer than it should have, but Qwin eventually located the switch buried deep behind a panel and flicked it to release the security latch. "There we go."

Eion kept his gaze locked on the transportation tube below as Qwin climbed through the hatch. It remained inert, even as Qwin reached out to take his hand to help him inside. "Scan for the women."

Qwin turned around as Eion placed the panel cover back in place. "There. Ten meters down that corridor. There's at least three armed guards inside and two out."

"They're clearly expecting us."

"Probably assumed they'd stop us before we got this far." Qwin looked up. "No word from Gadiel or Wex yet."

"Let's get into position." The moment the others were ready, Eion knew they'd have to move quickly.

It didn't take long for them to find an empty side room not far from where the women were being held. Qwin had grown hyper focused on a spot on the wall; no doubt, his mate was located in that direction. Inhibitor or not, his proximity to his mate was obviously impacting Qwin's ability to function. Eion had to assume that the others would respond in a similar manner, meaning he'd be the one with the greatest ability to see the bigger picture.

That was unnerving, mostly because he hadn't been able to fully push past his awareness of Kaia and how she was feeling. Every now and again he'd feel an emotional spike from her – fear, sadness, hope – which would cut through his attention on the matter before him. The sooner they saved the women, the sooner he could get back to Kaia and they could all get off this rock.

The soft beep of a communication being activated for a second before turning off, echoed in Eion's ear. He flicked his own communicator on in response, before pulling out a grenade. "They're in position."

They didn't need words to coordinate their attack; they'd done similar breaches more times than Eion could count. Qwin took up position on Eion's flank and they moved silently out of the room and into the corridor toward the guards. Eion paused and counted to three in his head before tossing the grenade blindly around the corner, sending it flying toward the men outside the door.

The explosion nearly coincided perfectly with the sound of an explosion inside the room, meaning Gadiel and Weixler had made their move as well. Eion and Qwin raced toward the chaos, through the smoke and into the room where the three guards were still alive and actively firing at Gadiel and Weixler. Qwin raced across the room to where a lone woman lay on the floor, a medical monitor knocked over on its side across her legs. Knowing that had to be Olya, Eion moved to lay suppressing fire, keeping both Qwin and Olya safe.

It was difficult to see Gadiel, Weixler, or the other women, leaving him to assume that they had matters on that side of the room under control. Qwin disconnected Olya from the monitors and lifted her into his arms. She struggled momentarily before her eyes appeared to focus on Qwin and she let out a soft. "Oh."

Eion realized there was no way Qwin would be able to get out of the building on his own, not without getting both him and his mate shot. "Move!"

Shooting anything that moved, Eion led Qwin out of the room back the way they'd come. By now, others had been alerted to their incursion, and the once empty corridors were now filled with Black Guard, preventing their escape. They were only on the second story and if they tried to make their way inside the building, they'd get caught or worse.

Grabbing Qwin's grenades, Eion scanned the outside wall for a weak spot. He secured all three to the wall and set a short timer. "Stand back."

"They'll have a shield up." Qwin pulled an unconscious Olya hard against his chest as they ducked into a room.

"One problem at a time."

The explosion rocked the building, but Eion wasted no time worrying about the inevitable attention. He began firing into the corridor, and then blindly shooting outside into the alleyway. The patrols had all come and were firing at the now exposed side, leaving them with little cover. They had erected a shield around the building, but it shimmered and quickly blipped out of existence. Gadiel and Weixler had clearly been successful in their tasks.

It only took a second for Eion's matrix to calculate the

distance to the ground. Qwin had two cybernetic legs and would be able to make the drop easily.

Eion would have more of a problem.

"Jump. I'll stay here and make sure you're covered."

Qwin peeked down, ensuring Olya stayed covered. "Are you sure?"

"Go!"

Qwin didn't question him again, instead getting a running start and leaping as far away from the building as he could manage. Eion fired both his blasters at the patrols until Qwin disappeared down an alley and hopefully to safety. Now he just needed to get out of here himself.

There weren't any conveniently placed boxes or buildings he could used to jump on, leaving him with few options. The longer he stayed here, the greater the likelihood he'd get caught. Eion did a quick scan and saw that some of the electrical cables where exposed from the explosion, offering him a way down. Jerking as many of the wires as he could, he wrapped the end of them around his hand, got a running start of his own and jumped out of the building. His momentum swung him out before redirecting him to the side of the building. Twisting in the air, he was able to get around in just enough time to plant his feet against the wall to stop himself, then let go of the cable and drop the rest of the way to the ground.

Pain lanced through his legs, but it wasn't enough to stop him from moving. Eion bolted in the opposite direction that Qwin had gone, hoping that if anyone were to follow it would buy the other cyborg more time to escape.

The next several minutes dissolved into a series of calculations; efficiency of blaster shots, distance of routes leading back to the shuttle, the speed by which his nanobots could repair the damage he'd taken from the fall. Eion easily slipped back into his role as second in command, emotionless and calculating. He began a search for Qwin and the others when something stopped him dead in his tracks.

Kaia.

Eion, help me!

The words were as clear in his head as if she were standing beside him. She was terrified, hurt, frantic to keep from getting pulled away by someone. Everything that had been at the forefront of Eion's mind vanished. Kaia was in danger and he had to get to her. Now.

Hold on - I'm coming!

Ignoring the danger before him, he bolted for her.

CHAPTER THIRTEEN

One moment Kaia was crouching behind the pilot's seat in a vain attempt to make herself as small as possible, and the next she was being yanked out of the shuttle by one of the red bug-men. How they'd known she was there she still wasn't certain. Nor did she know why the hell they'd wanted her out of the shuttle. She did her best not to scream out loud, instead praying Eion heard her silent, frantic pleas.

"What do we have here?" The tall woman sauntered around the front of the shuttle, looking at Kaia as though she were a snack. "I'm not familiar with your species."

Kaia bit her tongue, knowing that anything she'd say would no doubt get her into more trouble than she'd be able to handle. All she had to do was to play things smart and hold on long enough for Eion to come find her. Easy, right?

The woman moved so smoothly, Kaia would have thought she was on wheels. Her long purple hair rested over her shoulder as though it were a living thing that had simply laid down for a rest. Now that she was close enough to see her face closely, Kaia realized that the woman didn't have any color to her eyes, their black depths unnervingly set deeply in her iridescent face. The woman took Kaia's chin in her hands and lifted it up so she had no choice but the look the woman in the eyes.

"Aren't you an interesting creature." Her voice was lyrical, setting Kaia at ease. "What's your name?"

"Kaia." She hadn't meant to answer, but her name popped out of her without thinking.

"Kaia. You're speaking a language I'm not familiar with. What is it?"

"Earth standard." *No, no, no, stop talking you idiot.*

"Earth?" The woman looked over at one of her men, who shrugged his shoulders. "I'm not familiar with that planet either. You must have come quite the distance to be here."

"We did."

Panic raced through her when she realized that she was incapable of not responding to the woman. She must have realized what Kaia was thinking because she immediately grinned. "It's not your fault that you're speaking to me. Clearly, you're not familiar with my people or what we're capable of doing. Poor little thing. You're nothing more than a child lost in a world of scary monsters."

How had Kaia thought she'd be able to handle living a life out here on her own with Olya? This woman was right that she knew little of their new home, of this sector of space. She barely knew anything about Eion and his people, even if she felt safer with him than she had anywhere else in her life.

Eion.

If he didn't get her soon, she was going to be in trouble. More than she already was.

The woman ran her fingers through Kaia's hair. "So, Kaia from Earth, what exactly are you doing here? This doesn't seem like the sort of place you should be."

Kaia somehow forced her eyes closed and sucked in a deep breath before she bit down hard on her tongue. The words were lodged in her throat and for a second she thought she was going to spill every detail and put everyone at risk. But with her eyes shut it became easier for her to resist the pull of the woman's request and Kaia regained a small measure of her control.

"You're quite strong willed for a creature I've never heard of before. Fascinating."

Pain sliced through Kaia's side as something sharp cut through the fabric of her uniform and deep into her flesh. The subtle buzz of the nanobots in her body going to work to repair the damage were quickly washed away from the rush of pain far greater than anything she'd ever experienced. Gasping, she continued to force her eyes closed knowing if she were to open them once more, she'd have little chance of resisting the allure of the woman and her questions.

"I have to say that I'm impressed. Not many recognize that I need eye contact to gain psychic control over them." The woman pressed her fingers against Kaia's new wound, sending another burst of pain and pulling a cry from her. "I like such astute perception in a creature. It makes it far more entertaining when I break you."

"I don't think you're going to want to do that." Kaia focused her attention on Eion, mentally pushing out to him, praying he was on some level aware of what was happening to her. *Eion, help me!*

"Unless you're hiding some sort of poison on your body that I'm unaware of, my scans tell me you're no physical threat to me and certainly not to my boys. I don't believe there's a way you can stop me."

The soft growl of the bug-men sent a shiver through Kaia. With her eyes closed and not knowing exactly what they were doing, the sound was more menacing than when they'd pulled her from the shuttle. She knew they'd kill her if she gave them even the slightest reason to do so. It took effort not to squirm in the woman's grasp to attempt to break free.

Calm, you need to keep calm and buy time until Eion can help you.

"You Earthlings are emotional creatures, aren't you? Fear and despair are coming off you in delicious waves, making my skin tingle. I might have to tuck you away in my quarters so I can enjoy you for weeks." The woman moved her face close to Kaia's, the trickle of her breath across Kaia's cheek and throat were unnerving. "Until I get bored."

Kaia squeezed her eyes so hard the intensity of it made her scalp ache. "I don't think I'll be around that long." Eion needed to hurry the hell up so she wasn't proved a liar.

The woman made a sound that Kaia could only assume was a chuckle before she tossed her aside. The sudden rush of air against her face was met with the painful impact of landing hard on the ground. Kaia couldn't stop from opening her eyes to see what had happened, where she'd ended up. The gnarled and hardened face of one of the red bug-men appeared above her, wrenching a scream from her.

It made a clacking growl as it widened its mandibles and loomed closer. Kaia screamed again as she frantically kicked her feet, pumping her legs trying to pull back, away from its grasp. She couldn't look away from its opened mouth, from the massive claw-hands that were snapping as they reached for her. The press of the shuttle against her back was the only indication she had that her escape route had been effectively cut off.

The woman was laughing loudly, the maniacal cackle amping her fear up another notch. Her entire existence consisted of the bug-man, the smell of metal from the shuttle, and the creeping dread that she was going to die.

It was that dread that masked her initial awareness of Eion's arrival. When his thoughts finally broke through, they were cold and calculating.

Kaia. Kaia, I need you to listen to me.

Eion? She had no idea how they were able to communicate this way and given the circumstances, didn't particularly care. *Help!*

The bug-man snapped his claw-hand at her, snipping the air just above her arm. Kaia gasped as she rolled to the side away from him and the shuttle, scrambling for space. Her tenuous connection with Eion had faltered, leaving her only aware of his emotional state.

He was furious.

When a roar echoed across the landing pad, Kaia thought for a moment that it was the second bug-man coming to join his partner in apprehending her. But then the woman's screeches mixed with the sound of blaster fire and she knew that Eion had finally reached her. As the bug-man turned his attention to Eion, Kaia was able to frantically look around for something to help save them. The door to the shuttle had been destroyed, providing her with a path to safety. She looked up as Eion slammed his body fully into the second bug-man, sending them both crashing away from her.

Mentally yelling at herself to move, Kaia threw her body into the shuttle's cockpit and scrambled to fall into the pilot's seat. "Computer! Fire weapons!"

"Weapons unavailable due to planetary restrictions."

"I don't give a fuck about restrictions. Fire the lasers or whatever we have!"

"Weapons unavailable due to – "

"Shit."

She mashed the console's buttons hoping she'd be able to do something to help save Eion. He'd ducked behind some of the containers that the bug-men had dropped, avoiding the laser fire of the woman, who was retreating to her shuttle. So far, they hadn't seemed to have drawn the attention of the authorities, but Kaia knew that was only a matter of time. She had to stop the woman from getting to her ship and notifying anyone.

Eion roared once more as he threw himself at the closer of the two bug-men. This time he grabbed its claw-hand and with his unnatural strength, pulled at the creature, breaking its arm before he swiped at its leg and sent it crashing to the ground. It didn't put the creature down for long, but it gave Eion a moment to face her in the shuttle and point toward the container, before he was attacked by the second bug-man.

Yes, she could use the container to do…something, but she didn't exactly have weapons controls at the moment. Looking around, she had an idea. "Computer, what shuttle functions are available?"

"Flight, communications, limited tractor beam, area scans – "

"Wait, how limited is the tractor beam?"

"For use of loading and unloading supplies."

That must have been what Eion had meant when he'd pointed at the container. He wanted her to use the tractor beam and it as a weapon. Kaia stared down at the controls before looking once more at the woman with the purple hair and how close to her shuttle she'd gotten.

"Computer, I need to use the tractor beam to pick up the closest container."

A blue shimmering beam of light erupted from somewhere beneath the cockpit to envelop the larger of the three containers closest to the shuttle. "Bringing container into the cargo hold."

"No!" Kaia jumped to her feet as Eion was caught up by one of the bug-men and slammed repeatedly to the ground. The woman took that moment to make a break for her own ship, leaving Kaia with few options. "Computer, I need you to send that container as fast as you can to the other shuttle on this landing pad."

"That goes against standard operating – "

"I don't give a shit. Just do it!"

The container hovered in place for a moment, and then it shot like a missile toward the alien's shuttle, to crash against the side of the ship and stopping the woman dead in her tracks. She glared at Kaia, her mouth opening in what Kaia could only assume was a hiss before she changed direction and took cover behind the cargo mover.

"Computer, get another container. Where can I cause the most damage to the shuttle?"

"Analyzing." There was a soft hum in the cockpit, followed by a short beep. "The landing mechanism has a metallurgic fault that will prevent its retraction."

"Do that. Hit that there."

The computer didn't hesitate and sent another large container flying toward the vulnerable shuttle. What Kaia hadn't anticipated was the bug-man closest to the shuttle stepping in front of the projectile, smashing into it and sending him flying. The woman raced from her hiding spot but went to the bug-man's side with a wail, surprising Kaia. She could no longer see Eion, could only feel his anger and knew she needed to go to him.

He was beating the second bug-man with his cybernetic fist, slamming it on the creature's chest as it flailed around on the ground. He wore the same look of unbridled rage that he had back on Zarlan when the Black Guard had first attacked them and taken the others away. She knew in her heart he'd tear that creature limb from limb if she let him, all to keep her safe.

"Eion, stop!" She jumped out of the shuttle and raced to him, throwing herself on his back to pull him off. "Stop! You're killing him."

Unlike at the medical facility, this time he stopped the assault. Turning his face, she could see the wide-eyed fear he had, could feel his desperation at the thought of losing her. She awkwardly cupped his cheek and waited for his fear to recede before she kissed him softly. "I'm okay. No one hurt me."

Silence descended on them like a blanket, the lingering smell of blaster fire and blood hanging in the air. Eion closed his eyes and pulled in a deep breath before turning his attention back to the woman who was still slung across the body of the injured bug-man. Her purple hair was no longer neatly curled, the ends now splayed around her shoulders as she hissed at them. "You nearly killed my son."

"You attacked my mate. You're lucky I didn't do more."

The woman blinked slowly as she got to her feet, beckoning her other son to her side. "You're Fallen. They don't have *mates*."

"Yes they do. And we happen to be from Earth." Kaia squeezed Eion's shoulder when she felt him start to move. "We don't want any more trouble. Are we good here?"

The woman hissed once more. "I should report you to the Guard."

"You won't." Eion got to his feet, keeping Kaia pressed to his side. "You want to remain under their notice as much as we do."

"Really?" The woman lowered her chin to glare down at them. "Why is that?"

Eion pointed at one of the smashed containers. "You're loading food and medical supplies on a shuttle platform that's out of sensor range. Seeing as your manifest says that you're unloading supplies, that means you're running a side business. I can't imagine the Guard would be happy to find out that you're cutting them out of their share of the market. I recommend getting your children on your ship and leave before we both get caught."

She hesitated, looking down at her children briefly before brushing her hands together. "On the ship. Now."

Kaia couldn't tear her gaze away from the woman, would probably have run to her side if it hadn't been for Eion's iron grip on her. "We should go with them. We can use her ship to leave."

"That's the last place either of us want to end up." Only once the door to the other shuttle slid shut and the engines powered up did Eion let go of her. "She's a Va'nita. They feed off emotional energy, which is one of the reasons why they don't like being in the presence of Fallen. We're not exactly known for our emotional responses."

"Except for anger." With the woman now gone, Kaia's head felt clearer than it had been in hours. She shifted so she could get a better look at him. "I don't need to be an empath to have felt how angry you were."

"They were trying to harm you. I heard your cries for help all the way back at the building." He lifted his hand to touch her but stopped short. "We've only known of one another for such a short time and yet I know I'd destroy a world to keep you safe."

Kaia bit her lower lip. "You would?"

"Foolish woman. Of course, I would." There was an intensity to his gaze that went far beyond the synthetic glow of his eyes. She saw the rage, the possession, and something she wanted to hope was love shining back at her as a small smile turned his lips.

Her heart shattered into a million pieces, only to fuse back together stronger than before. It was in that moment that she remembered something her mother had said to her long ago when Kaia had asked her about having enough love for her twins.

The beautiful thing about love is that it doesn't diminish from being shared. It multiplies and makes the bearer of that love all the stronger for its growth.

Swallowing past the lump of emotions that constricted her throat, Kaia refocused. "Olya. Is she okay? Where are the others?"

"Qwin has your sister and should be back here soon. We were separated from Weixler, Gadiel and the other women."

She wanted to ask him a million more questions – were they safe, would they be able to escape the planet, was Olya going to be okay – but the words refused to come. She knew in her heart this was the worst possible time to focus on anything other than getting the hell out of here. But with the slash down across Eion's shoulder and chest, oozing blood across his shirt and down his exposed cybernetic arm, she made him the priority.

"You're hurt." Stepping close, she pressed her hand against the wound. "We need to get you cleaned up."

"The nanobots will fix me."

"Inside the shuttle. Now." He didn't argue, instead letting her pull him along inside. "Sit."

Eion did as he was told, silently lifting his arms when she pulled his shirt off, giving her a better look at the injury. The nanobots had indeed already begun the work, as his skin stitched itself back together before her eyes.

"I told you, I was okay." This time he didn't stop from taking her face in his hands and pulling her in for a kiss.

The moment they touched, Kaia's panic subsided. He'd come to save her, he'd done everything possible to save her sister, been there fully and completely for her. While everything might be new and confusing, this at least was starting make sense. He was starting to make sense. Eion was fiercely brave, loyal and protective of anyone who he cared for. His warmth encompassed her inside and out.

The press of his mouth grew harder and there was no going back. It didn't matter where they were or what was happening around them, she needed him. Pulling back just far enough to be able to look him in the eyes, she whispered. "Make love to me."

She didn't need to ask twice.

CHAPTER FOURTEEN

Eion's cock was painfully hard as he pulled Kaia down on his lap, relieved that somehow, they'd both escaped the attack in one piece. Never in his life or since his rebirth had he been that terrified about losing another person. When he'd rounded the corner to see Kaia pressed against the shuttle and the Va'nita male moving in to harm her, everything else fell away and all he could think was that he was going to lose her before they'd even had the chance to start a life together.

She could die and he hadn't been there for her.

Holding her close, the surge of sexual energy was so strong he couldn't stop from pulling at her clothing, needing to see her skin to ensure she wasn't hurt, that she was whole. The press of her naked skin against his both soothed his fears and ignited his passion. Kaia was here, against all odds and everything that had been thrown at them over the past two days, she was here with him. Here for him as much as he was for her.

"Eion." She sighed his name against his lips before taking his mouth with hers.

He slid his hands down her back, cataloguing every nick and scratch with his fingers, until he cupped her ass to squeeze hard.

Kaia shifted so she now fully straddled him, her opening pressed against his cock, her weight squeezing down on his *rondella* until he thought he'd go mad from desire. He wanted to speak, to tell her that he loved her more than anything else in the world, but the words refused to form on his tongue. Instead, he deepened the kiss as he captured her breast in his hand to squeeze and tease the sensitive flesh until she moaned.

His entire life, Eion had wanted nothing more than to be needed by someone, wanted to be useful and care for others. He'd dedicated his entire life to the service of his people, never asking for anything in return. On the nights when he'd lain alone in his bed, silent in contemplation about what his life had become, never had he considered that the universe would grant him this beautiful gift – that Kaia would find him through the darkness of space.

Kaia pulled back with a gasp, her face still hovering just above his. "Eion." She cupped his face, her fingers stroking his beard. "I…this is…"

He knew she wanted to say the words that he too felt in his heart. He felt her confusion as much as her love, which was something he could address the only way he knew how. "I love you. This is strange and confusing, how our people have come together. I'm not certain anyone understands what's happening. All I am aware of is for the first time since my rebirth, I *feel* again. Truly feel emotions. Love, fear, joy, states of my being that I'd been told were lost to me because of the rebirth process. Your presence has done more to change my life than anything else ever has. I love you for that."

Tears streaked down her cheeks as he spoke, her eyes wide open and her lips parted. "In my world if you tell someone else that you love them without an appropriate period having passed, others will sometimes call you a fool. What I feel for you doesn't feel foolish, or wrong. It feels like for the first time in my life, I have something that is all my own. That you and I are exactly the right thing. I love you too."

With the words between them now spoken, it was as though a breaker was tripped and they were free to show one another how they felt. Eion got to his feet, taking Kaia with him, and laid her down on the floor. They had no time for seduction, only the physical affirmation and reassurance that they were both here and alive. She pulled her pants down without taking them off and rolled to her hands and knees, presenting herself to him. Eion wasted no time pushing his pants down, lining his cock up with her entrance and pushing himself forward until he was fully inside.

They both groaned as he took her hips in his hands, pulled back and slammed into her once more. Kaia shivered, her muscles clenching around his cock as goosebumps formed across her skin. "Yes, hard like that."

That was good, because he knew he wouldn't be able to hold back, to be gentle and loving the way she deserved. Immediately, he set an unrelenting pace, knowing they'd both be brought to the precipice of pleasure far faster than either would have liked. Later, he'd kiss every inch of her skin, worship her body, and read the story that it told of her sacrifices and life.

Kaia lowered her upper body to the floor, reached between her legs and pressed her fingers against his *rondella*, yanking a surprised gasp from him. The rush of pleasure from a pre-orgasm also caught him by surprise, coming far faster than he would have liked. No, he wasn't going to give in to the pleasure just yet, not when Kaia hadn't come undone around him.

Leaning forward so he was now draped across her back, he supported his weight with his cybernetic arm and reached between her legs with the other. Finding the soft, sensitive core easily, he pressed and rubbed small circles against her clit, loving the low moans and soft gasps the touch elicited. He slowed his thrusts so he could better time them with his touch against her, knowing how close to her pleasure she'd come.

"Harder," she begged, and he was more than happy to comply.

Increasing the pressure against her clit, he bit down on the back of her shoulder, wanting once more to mark her, announcing yet again to the world that Kaia was his, that he'd kill and die for her. The mix of dual sensations was enough to push her over the edge, the cries of her release filling the small cabin of the shuttle. He felt her orgasm as though it were his own, heating his cells and sending shivers of pleasure through his body.

Eion held back until he felt that she'd reached her peak and was starting to become overwhelmed. Only then did he withdraw his hand to lean back and recapture her hips. He loved this woman and knew that nothing in his life would ever be the same again. With his eyes closed, Eion let his love flow out of him as he burned deep into his matrix everything that was Kaia. When she once more reached between her legs and pressed against his *rondella*, he didn't try to hold back. His pleasure slammed into him and he pushed out the sensations with his mind, hoping she'd be able to experience even a fraction of what he felt the way he had with her. Kaia's gasp and the sudden shivers and twitches of her body told him that she must have, which brought about another wave of his orgasm.

What he hadn't expected was the marking scent that erupted from his *rondella* to fill the air and tell any Grus or Fallen that Kaia was his mate and his alone. His orgasm heightened again, pushing him nearly to the point of blacking out and ripping a scream from his chest.

Finally, it subsided and Eion lost the ability to move. They fell together in a half-naked heap on the floor of the shuttle, wrapped in each other's arms.

"Fuck." Her breathing was soft against his chest. "That was intense."

"Later, when we have time and are safe, I promise to do that again only slower. I will bring you so much pleasure you'll be unable to stand for days."

Kaia laughed. "I haven't felt safe in a long time."

"You are. I'll ensure nothing bad ever happens to you." He pushed her hair from her eyes and tilted her chin, so she'd look up at him. "I love you."

"I love you too."

A noise from outside the shuttle reminded him that they weren't out of harm's way quite yet. With regret he'd never felt before, Eion sat up. "The others will be here soon. We need to get ready to fly."

"The door to the shuttle is destroyed." She got dressed as she spoke, and unlike the first time they'd made love, there wasn't any awkwardness or emotional hurt. "How are we going to survive orbit?"

That was an excellent question. "I'll have to figure something out."

Now that he was back with Kaia, and that they'd truly mated, Eion was able to think clearly. "We need to find a panel that I can weld in place once the others arrive. We won't have long to do so, and I'll need to reprogram the shuttle's shields to reinforce that area. If we take any laser fire once we're in orbit, we're dead."

"Wonderful. Not out of the fire yet then." Kaia looked outside. "Still no sign of the others. I thought you said Qwin and Olya were on their way?"

"He left the building before me. I'd expected them back here before myself." He tried to reach out through the cybernetic link, but the inhibitors must still be functioning because he received nothing but static in response. "We have to assume they'll be here soon and need to be ready."

"Do you think we can use some of the shielding that fell off the other ship when they took off?" She pointed to something just out of his field of vision. "There looks to be a piece that's big enough."

"Stay here. I'll grab something so we can get out of here quickly."

It didn't take long for him to find a single sheet of metal that would cover the door. Though this wasn't ideal, and they'd be forced to find another shuttle that was secure enough to get them all the way back to Zarlan, at least it should hold long enough to get them away from the grasp of the Black Guard. Time wasn't on their side and the longer it took for Qwin and the others to return, the more Eion had to consider the fact that he and Kaia might have to leave alone.

He didn't know how she'd respond to the thought of needing to trust Qwin to look after her sister.

It took effort to get the metal into place and ready to be welded to the ship, but he managed to do so as the sounds of a commotion reached him. Even though their cybernetic link still wasn't working, he knew that was Qwin with Olya and that they were coming with a Black Guard patrol fast on their feet.

"Kaia, start the shuttle. Now."

"What's happening?"

"Now!"

With his gaze locked on the far end of the landing pad, Eion continued to ping Qwin through the link, hoping they'd be able to force some sort of connection. As the other cyborg rounded the corner and came into visual range, Eion had to strain before finally hearing Qwin's words.

Start the shuttle!

Already started. How many?

Qwin's relief was palpable. *Three patrols. Ran into Weixler and Petra but got separated again.*

We might not be able to wait for them. The shuttle is damaged, and we need to leave.

Qwin's response was cut off by the distant sound of blaster fire. They'd have time to talk once they were safely onboard the ship and launched into orbit. Eion had his blaster out and aimed at the still empty spot where Qwin was heading, silently counting down the remaining distance until they made it to safety. *Ten meters, nine, eight...*

"Qwin and Olya are coming."

He felt Kaia's relief before she even spoke. "Thank god."

They reached the shuttle with still no sign of the Black Guard patrol arriving. If things went their way, Weixler and Petra might also reach them before they'd need to leave. Eion moved aside and let Qwin climb onboard, Olya in his arms. "Any sign of Gadiel?"

"None. Weixler said he hasn't seen him or his mate since they escaped the roof."

"*Frak.*" Eion knew Gadiel well enough to know that if there was even the slightest chance that they wouldn't make it back to the shuttle, he'd want Eion to leave without him. They'd find another way off the planet. "Wex better hurry."

"I'm not able to reach him through the link either. He should be close." It only took a moment for Qwin to be brought up to speed on the state of the shuttle and the perilous nature of their escape.

Kaia was out from the cockpit and to her sister's side. "Olya! Is she okay?"

"She will be. I gave her a sedative to help after our escape." Qwin looked down at the woman in his arms with a grimace. "I need medical supplies to help her that I don't have access to here. We'll need to find a place to put down long before we reach Zarlan."

"Shit." The quiver in Kaia's voice betrayed her fears. "I'd hoped the nanobots would be enough to cure her Breneman's virus."

"Almost."

Their peace was shattered at the sound of blaster fire just outside of the shuttle. Eion leaned out of the shuttle to return fire and counted two full patrols. "Time's up."

"But the others aren't back yet." Kaia raced back to the cockpit.

"They'll have to find another way off planet." Eion moved the metal into place while Qwin secured Olya in the bed.

"We should give them more time."

Frak, he wished they could. "Kaia, our hull is damaged and won't survived a barrage of blaster fire. We have to get the shields up and get out of here." As though to punctuate his point, the shuttle rattled as the smell of heated metal filled the compartment as the blaster fire continued.

He hated that he felt her hesitation and guilt as she did as he asked, but none of them had time to worry about the consequences. Either some of them escaped or none of them did, and Eion wouldn't be able to live with himself if he hadn't done everything in his power to save those he could. The shuttle rocked as blaster fire continued to pelt them before Kaia was able to get the shields to full. That bought them a brief respite, but they needed to take off as soon as they could or run the risk of another better armed patrol arriving.

Qwin joined him and together they used the onboard emergency lasers to weld the panel to the shuttle. Thankfully, their cybernetic vision ensured that they were able to make the seal solid enough that along with the shield, they'd be able to survive the liftoff through the atmosphere.

"Eion, get up here."

He tossed the laser to the side and raced to the cockpit as Kaia was pointing at the group of Black Guard who were now firing both at the shuttle and at something off to the side. He felt Weixler's presence through the cybernetic link. "Shit."

"It's them, isn't it." Kaia's face drained of color. "Is it too late to get them on board?"

"There's too many people between us and them." Focusing his attention, he reached out through the link. *Wex?*

It was fuzzy initially, but after a moment he heard the other cyborg. *We're pinned down. Need suppressing fire to make it to you.*

The shuttle is damaged. We needed to weld the door shut.

There was a pause and for a heartbeat Eion feared the worst before Weixler came back. *I see another shuttle. I'll get her out on that.*

Gad?

No sign of him.

He'll figure something out. I'll lay down fire so you can run. We'll meet up on Zarlan.

Good luck.

You too.

"He's getting Petra out on another ship." Kaia slipped out of the pilot's seat and into the co-pilot chair so Eion could take control. "Qwin, is Olya ready to – "

"Fly! I've got her."

Eion waited until Kaia was secured before grinning at her. "Hold on."

Then chaos erupted.

CHAPTER FIFTEEN

Kaia knew she should be absolutely terrified about the mere fact they were firing down on hostile forces while trying to escape a planet on a ship that had no business flying, let alone going into space. But when Eion looked at her and grinned, she couldn't help but laugh, swept up in his infectious joy.

If someone had told her before she'd boarded the Kraken back on Earth that this was what her life was going to be, she would never have believed them.

Her stomach bottomed out from the sudden liftoff of the shuttle and the quick turn around as Eion moved it to face their attackers.

"Computer, return fire. Concentrate on sector three-zero-nine-two."

"Acknowledged."

She could only hope whatever they were able to do was enough to help Weixler and Petra get to the safety of another ship and make their own escape. Shit, they might need to meet up with them and hitch a ride if their patch job didn't last long enough for them to make it to Zarlan. She had a dozen questions she wanted to ask but held her peace, not wanting to be a distraction.

The shuttle rattled and shook, sending her back hard against her seat. "That didn't feel right."

"They've brought out a laser cannon. We can't stay here." Eion looked back at Qwin. "He's got your sister secured."

"What about Wex and Petra?"

Eion cocked his head to the side. "They're in their shuttle. That's all we can do for them." Without another word, he spun the shuttle around and entered a series of commands into the console. "Hold on."

Unlike their entry, everyone was aware of them and their escape, which meant there was no way to conceal their departure from the Black Guard. Kaia didn't know the first thing about piloting a shuttle, but even she could appreciate Eion's maneuvers as he dodged incoming fire and the steady stream of ships entering and leaving the atmosphere.

The computer beeped and he quickly pressed several more buttons. "They're trying to lock on with a tractor beam. Computer, evasive maneuvers. Bring us in close to one of the bigger frigates if necessary."

"Acknowledged."

Kaia's head and stomach were once more rattled by the sudden change in direction. She wasn't normally one to get motion sickness, but this was pushing even her iron constitution to the limit. Looking back toward where Qwin and her sister were, she could only hope Olya was handling the unexpected jolts okay. Shit, Kaia should have gone back there to be with her. She was useless in the co-pilot's seat, Qwin being the much better option to help Eion if needed. Looking after Olya was something she knew how to do, something she could control. Something that –

She's not your responsibility anymore.

The thought hit her harder than the latest jolt from the shuttle's escape. It wasn't that she was handing off responsibility for her sister to someone else. Kaia knew it was never her place to have taken on that responsibility. Coming to this realization while there was a strong possibility that they might all die, was probably the worst bout of timing she'd ever had in her life.

Eion swerved their shuttle so it flew directly beneath a frigate, and the laser fire stopped. "That will buy us some time." He pressed additional commands into the console. "I'm going to try and sneak us out of here."

"How?"

"Like this."

With a press of a button, their shuttle leaped forward at an accelerated rate, only to come to a dead stop beneath a second large frigate. He then moved them in another accelerated leap next to a third, much smaller vessel. Then a fourth, and fifth until they were halfway around the sector, having leap-frogged their way, hiding in the other ships' sensor dark spots. Kaia sat open mouthed watching, the excitement she felt coming off him infectious.

"That was amazing." She turned to look at him straight on. "Will they be able to track us?"

"Not from the surface. But they've already sent up ships to visually scan for us. We need to get out of here."

Rather than bolt out of the region the way she would have assumed, Eion instead slowly shifted their shuttle so it blended in with a larger group of ships leaving orbit and spreading out in various directions of the sector. With all the leaping they'd done, it would take far too long for the Black Guard to visually identify which shuttle was theirs and follow them to their destination.

"You're fucking brilliant." Ignoring his protests as she stood, Kaia leaned in and kissed his cheek. "I love you."

Eion's grin was all the response she needed.

Moving her mouth to his ear, she sucked his lobe hard into her mouth before scraping it against her teeth as she slowly let it go. "When all this is over. When we're back safe on Zarlan and Olya is healed, I'm going to take you up on that offer to not get out of bed for days. I want a life of my own and I want to spend it with you."

His soft growl sent a shiver through her. "Be careful what you ask for."

"Do you think we're okay? I want to check on Olya."

He pulled up the scanner and nodded. "That might change quickly, but I don't see anyone following us yet. Strap in back there and send Qwin up."

"I will." She gave him another kiss before making her way to the back of the shuttle.

Olya had opened her eyes and was looking warily at Qwin. Kaia knew that expression better than most, having been on the receiving end more than once. Something had happened between them and Olya was far from pleased. Qwin stood the moment Kaia drew close, giving her space by the bed. "She's stable for now."

"Eion asked if you'd join him – "

"Of course." He left without letting her finish.

Kaia watched him stride the short distance to the front of the shuttle before claiming his former seat for herself. "What was that about?"

"Nothing."

It was most definitely not *nothing*, but Kaia wasn't a fool and knew there was no point in pressing her twin if she didn't want to talk about what had happened. Brushing Olya's hair from her face, Kaia looked her sister over. "How are you feeling?"

"Tired. Confused. It's like…I've barely had time to catch my breath since coming out of stasis and I've already been kidnapped, drugged and told that I now apparently have a life mate." She snorted as she rolled her eyes. "All I wanted was a cure for this frigging disease."

"We'll find one. Qwin was saying that the nanobots should be able to help keep everything at bay. At least until they can find a more permanent cure."

Olya looked away, her gaze locked on the ceiling. "I don't know if I trust him."

"Why not?" Kaia took her sister's hand in hers, squeezing it hard. "Did he do something to you? Are you hurt?"

She couldn't imagine Eion or the others doing anything to harm their mates, especially as her mental connection with him grew deeper. But she also knew Olya wasn't prone to overreactions and if she didn't trust Qwin, then something must have happened during their escape from where she'd been held prisoner. And yet, when Olya looked back at her, eyes wide and slightly panicked, she realized it must be something else.

"No, no, not like that. I don't think he's capable of hurting anyone." She huffed. "It's just, we don't know anything about these people, and we're supposed to simply accept the idea that they're our mates *forever*? I can't believe you're going along with this without an argument."

Kaia found herself looking down the length of the shuttle at Eion. She didn't need to see his face to feel his affection for her, his determination to ensure that he'd get them all to safety, and his fierce intelligence as he plotted their escape. She knew that despite the improbability of it all, they'd found their way to the exact place they needed to be.

"Wow. I guess you do believe it."

She looked down at Olya and smiled. "It's been an interesting few days."

"You'll have to tell me all about it when we get back to wherever the hell we're going."

"As long as you fill me in on what happened to you since you've been kidnapped."

Olya laughed. "It really has been a crazy few – "

The shuttle shook violently, and Kaia's hair whipped around

toward where the shuttle door was. Alarms blared and it suddenly became difficult to breathe.

Oh shit, the patch didn't hold. They were going to die.

"Kaia!" Olya clung to her hand as Olya began to convulse.

No, no, no, not now. Not when they were so close to freedom, to having a life giving them everything Kaia wanted.

"Hold on!" Eion was at the door, using the welder to secure the leak and as quickly as the chaos began, it was over. "Is everyone okay?"

Qwin was already back with a medical scanner, injecting something into Olya as Kaia could only watch. "The nanobots aren't able to keep up with whatever they did to Olya."

"Wait, what?" She got to her feet and pulled on Qwin's shoulder until he looked her in the eye. "I thought this was just the Breneman's. What did they do to her?"

"I don't know." She didn't need to have a mental connection to Qwin to feel his rage. "But I'm *fraking* well going to find out."

Eion appeared behind her. "This shuttle isn't going to make it back to Zarlan. The shields were weakened by the laser fire we took, and the patch isn't going to survive given the stress on it with traveling."

"I need a medical facility so I can run some scans and see exactly what's going on with Olya's body." Qwin pinched the bridge of his nose. "Her condition has deteriorated far faster than I would expect given the nanobots in her bloodstream."

"I'll find us a location where we can put down, get a new ship and find whatever you need to help her." Eion pulled Kaia in for a hug and some of her fears lessened. "Don't worry. Either of you. We'll get through this."

Qwin nodded. "I'm going to stay with her to ensure she's stable."

"I'll let you know when I find a location." Eion gave her one final squeeze before letting her go.

Kaia found herself following him to the front of the shuttle. "Will we? Get through this?"

Rather than simply offer her a verbal reassurance, he pulled her into another hug and held her tightly. "I know this means nothing to you, but we're the Qadrus. Impossible tasks are our speciality. We'll save your sister and get back to Zarlan."

"Promise?"

"I do." He kissed the tip of her nose. "I have no doubt that Weixler and Gadiel will be there waiting, wondering what took us so long."

She could feel how strongly he believed his words. That reassurance was all Kaia needed. If they were strong as a team of four, then they'd be unstoppable as a group of eight. Looking into his glowing green eyes, she smiled. "Then let's get to it."

ACKNOWLEDGMENTS

Thank you everyone for reading **EION**, book one in my new interconnected Cyborg Rogues series. You can pre-order **QWIN** now on Amazon. Haven't had enough Eion and Kaia? Sign up for my newsletter to receive **a free bonus chapter**! Want to read the book that started it all? **CONSUMED BY THE CYBORG** is available now from Amazon and KU!

ALSO BY ALYSE ANDERS

Cyborg Protectors – Origins

Consumed by the Cyborg
Mated to the Cyborg
Saved by the Cyborg
Healed by the Cyborg

Cyborg Protectors – Prison

Chained to the Cyborg
Freed by the Cyborg
Exposed by the Cyborg
Redeemed by the Cyborg

Cyborg Rogues

Eion
Qwin
Weixler
Gadiel

ABOUT THE AUTHOR

Alyse Anders is the author of the Cyborg Protector series of erotic sci-fi novellas. When she's not sitting in front of her computer with her imagination stuck in a far away nebula, she's at home with her husband and two dogs, usually eating far too much chocolate for her own good. Check out more of Alyse's books on Amazon and KU or visit her website **www.alyseanders.com**.

Made in the USA
Middletown, DE
21 April 2021